Who is Jerry Cornelius? First mentioned by Virgil in the first century B.C., he crops up again in the Boer War, when a dispatch dated 1900 shows him to have been shot in the Transvaal. But he's still around (and possibly always was), an immortal, ubiquitous assassin who has himself been the subject of assassination attempts by his brother Frank – and of novels by Michael Moorcock.

Who he is, or how, where, when or why, we shall probably never know. However, the stories collected in this book provide a picaresque and kaleidoscopic biography of this enigmatic and sinister superhero, whose adventures in Mandalay, London, the Vatican and elsewhere make a non-sense of the here and now, a satire of our times and of time itself.

THE LIVES AND TIMES OF
JERRY CORNELIUS

Q ———————————————————

MICHAEL MOORCOCK

Illustrated by Mal Dean, Richard Glyn Jones
and Harry Douthwaite

QUARTET BOOKS   LONDON

Published by Quartet Books Limited 1976
27 Goodge Street, London W1P 1FD
First published by Alison and Busby Limited 1976

Copyright © 1976 by Michael Moorcock

ISBN 0 704 31264 6

Printed in Great Britain by
Richard Clay (The Chaucer Press) Ltd,
Bungay, Suffolk

Acknowledgements

"The Peking Junction" originally appeared in *The New SF*, edited by Langdon Jones, Hutchinson, 1969. "The Delhi Division", "The Tank Trapeze" and "The Nature of the Catastrophe" first appeared in *New Worlds Magazine*, 1968, 1969, 1970. "The Swastika Set-Up" first appeared in *Corridor* edited and published by Michael Butterworth, 1972. "The Sunset Perspective" first appeared in an anthology edited by George Hay, Panther, 1971. "Sea Wolves" first appeared in *Science Against Man*, edited by Anthony Cheetham, Avon, 1970. "Voortrekker" first appeared in *Quark*, No.4, edited by Delany and Hucker, 1971. "Dead Singers" appeared in *Ink*, 1971. "The Longford Cup" first appeared in *Penthouse*, 1973. "The Entropy Circuit" first appeared in *An Index of Possibilities*, 1974. The stories are published in order of writing, and should be read as a continuous narrative.

The illustrations for "The Delhi Division" and "The Tank Trapeze" are by Mal Dean, for "The Longford Cup" and "The Entropy Circuit" by Richard Glyn Jones, and for "The Swastika Set-Up" by Harry Douthwaite.

Contents

"Freedom of thought and action is this century's most terrible gift to Western civilisation, our most fearful burden. I for one would gladly relinquish that burden." – Lobkowitz, 1965

The
Peking
Junction

1

Out of the rich and rolling lands of the west came Jerry
Cornelius, with a vibragun holstered at his hip and a generous
message in his heart, to China.

Six feet two inches tall, rather fat, dressed in the beard and
uniform of a Cuban guerrilla, only his eyes denied his appearance
or, when he moved, his movements. Then the uniform was seen
for what it was and those who at first had admired him loathed
him and those who had at first despised him loved him. He loved
them all, for his part, he kissed them all.

On the shores of a wide lake that reflected the full moon stood a tall, ruined pagoda, its walls inlaid with faded mosaic of red, pale blue and yellow. In the dusty room on the first floor Jerry poured Wakayama Sherry for three disconcerted generals whose decision to meet him in this remote province had been entirely a matter of instinct.

"Substantial," murmured one general, studying the glass.

Jerry watched the pink tongue travel between the lips and disappear in the left-hand corner of the mouth.

"The tension," began a second general carefully. "The tension."

Jerry shrugged and moved about the room very swiftly. He came to rest on the mat in front of them, sat down, folded his legs under him.

A winged shadow crossed the moon. The third general glanced at the disintegrating mosaic of the wall. "Only twice in . . ."

Jerry nodded tolerantly.

For Jerry's sake they were all speaking good Mandarin with a certain amount of apprehensive self-contempt, like collaborators who fear reprisals from their countrymen.

"How is it now, over there?" asked one of the generals, waving towards the west.

"Wild and easy," said Jerry, "as always."

"But the American bombing . . ."

"A distraction, true." Jerry scratched his palm.

The first general's eyes widened. "Paris razed, London gutted, Berlin in ruins . . ."

"You take a lot from your friends before you condemn them."

Now the shadow had vanished. The third general's right hand spread its long fingers wide. "But the destruction . . . Dresden and Coventry were nothing. Thirty days – skies thick with Yankee pirate jets, constant rain of napalm, millions dead." He sipped his sherry. "It must have seemed like the end of the world . . ."

Jerry frowned. "I suppose so." Then he grinned. "There's no point in making a fuss about it, is there? Isn't it all for the best in the long run?"

The general looked exasperated. "You people . . ."

2

Tension, resulting in equilibrium: the gestures of conflict keep the peace. A question of interpretation.

3

Having been Elric, Asquiol, Minos Aquilinus, Clovis Marca, now and forever he was Jerry Cornelius of the noble price, proud prince of ruins, boss of the circuits. Faustaff, Muldoon, the eternal champion . . .

Nothing much was happening in the Time Centre that day; phantom horsemen rode on skeletal steeds across worlds as fantastic as those of Bosch or Breughel, and at dawn when clouds of giant scarlet flamingoes rose from their nests of reeds and wheeled through the sky in bizarre ritual dances, a tired, noble figure would go down to the edge of the marsh and stare over the water at the strange configurations of dark lagoons and tawny islands that seemed to him like hieroglyphs in some primaeval language. (The marsh had once been his home, but now he feared it his tears filled it.)

Cornelius feared only fear and had turned his albino beast from the scene, riding sadly away, his long mane flowing behind him so that from a distance he resembled some golden-haired madonna of the lagoons.

4

Imposition of order upon landscape; the romantic vision of the age of reason, the age of fear. And yet the undeniable rhythm of the spheres, the presence of God. The comforts of tidiness; the almost unbearable agony of uncompromising order. Law and Chaos. The face of God, the core of self :

"For the mind of man alone is free to explore the lofty vastness of the cosmic infinite, to transcend ordinary consciousness, or roam the secret corridors of the brain where past and future melt into one. . . . And universe and individual are linked, the one mirrored in the other, and each contains the other." – *The Chronicle of the Black Sword*

5

It was extremely subtle, he thought, staring out of the window at the waters of the lake. In another room, the generals slept. The appearance of one thing was often almost exactly that of its diametric opposite. The lake resembled a spread of smoothed silver; even the reeds were like wires of pale gold and the sleeping herons could have been carved from white jade. Was this the ultimate mystery? He checked his watch. Time for sleep.

6

In the morning the generals took Cornelius to the site of the crashed F111A. It was in fair condition, with one wing buckled and the tailplane shot away, its ragged pilot still at his controls, a dead hand on the ejector lever. The plane stood in the shadow of the cliff, half-hidden from the air by an overhang. Jerry was reluctant to approach it.

"We shall expect a straight answer," said a general.

"Straight," said Jerry, frowning. It was not his day.

"What was the exact nature of the catastrophe?" enquired one general of another.

Jerry forced himself to climb up on to the plane's fuselage and strike a pose he knew would impress the generals. It was becoming important to speed things up as much as he could.

"What do you mean by that?" The general raised his eyes to him, but Jerry was not sure that he had been addressed. "What does it mean to you, Mr Cornelius?"

Jerry felt cornered. "Mean?" He ran his hand over the pitted metal, touching the USAF insignia, the star, the disc, the bar.

"It will go in the museum eventually," said the first general, "with the fifty-eight Thunderbird, of course, and the rest, But what of the land?" A gesture towards the blue-green plain which spread away beyond their parked jeeps. "I do not understand."

Jerry pretended to study the cliff. He didn't want the generals to see him weeping.

Later they all piled into the jeep and began to roar away across the dusty plain, protecting their mouths and eyes with their scarves.

Returning to the pagoda by the lake, one of the generals stared thoughtfully back across the flat landscape. "Soon we shall have all this in shape."

The general touched a square object in one uniform pocket. The sound of a raucous Chinese brass band began to squall out. Herons flapped from the reeds and rose into the sky.

"You think we should leave the plane where it is, don't you?" said General Way Hahng.

Cornelius shrugged. But he had made contact, he thought complacently.

7

The heavy and old-fashioned steam locomotive shunted to a stop. Behind it the rickety carriages jostled together for a moment before coming to rest. Steam rose beneath the locomotive and the Chinese engineer stared pointedly over their heads at the plain as they clambered from the jeep and approached the train.

A few peasants occupied the carriages. Only one stared briefly through the window before turning his head away. The peasants, men and women, wore red overalls.

Walking knee-deep through the clammy steam they got into the carriage immediately behind the tender. The locomotive began to move.

Jerry sprawled across the hard bamboo seat and picked a splinter from his sleeve. In the distance he could see hazy mountains. He glanced at General Way Hahng but the general was concentrating on loosening a belt buckle. Jerry craned his head back and spotted the jeep, abandoned beside the rails.

He switched on his visitaper, focusing it on the window. Shadowy figures began to move on the glass, dancing to the music which had filled the carriage. The generals were surprised but said nothing. The tune was *Hello Goodbye*, by the Beatles.

It was not appropriate. Jerry turned it off. There again, he thought, perhaps it was appropriate. Every plugged nickel had two sides.

He burst into laughter.

General Way Hahng offered him a swift, disapproving glance, but no more.

"I hear you are called the Raven in the west," said another general.

"Only in Texas," said Jerry, still shaking.

"Aha, in *Texas*."

General Way Hahng got up to go to the lavatory. Jacket removed, the general's tight pants could be seen to stretch over beautifully rounded buttocks. Jerry looked at them feeling ecstatic. He had never seen anything like them. The slightly rumpled material added to their attraction.

"And in Los Angeles?" said another general. "What are you called in Elay?"

"Fats," said Jerry.

8

"Even though he was a physicist, he knew that important biological objects come in pairs." – Watson, *The Double Helix*

"With sinology, as with Chinese food, there are two *kinds* . . ."
– Enright, *Encounter*, July 1968

9

General Lee met them at the station. It was little more than a wooden platform raised between the railroad line and the Yellow River.

He shook hands with Jerry. "My apologies," he said. "But under the circumstances I thought it would be better to meet here than in Weifang."

"How much time have you got?" Jerry asked.

General Lee smiled and spread his hands. "You know better than that, Mr Cornelius." They walked to where the big Phantom IV staff car was parked.

General Way Hahng called from the window as the train moved off. "We will go on to Tientsin and journey back from there. We will wait for you, Mr Cornelius."

Jerry waved reassuringly.

General Lee was dressed in a neat Ivy League suit that was a little shiny, a little frayed on one sleeve. He was almost as tall as Jerry, with a round face, moody eyes and black chin whiskers. He returned his driver's salute as he personally opened the door of the limousine for Jerry. Jerry got in.

They sat in the stationary car and watched the river. General Lee put a hand on Jerry's shoulder. Jerry smiled back at his friend.

"Well," said the general eventually, "what do you think?"

"I think I might be able to do it. I think I'm building something up there. With Way Hahng."

Lee rubbed at the corner of his mouth with his index finger. "Yes. I thought it would be Way Hahng."

"I can't promise anything," Jerry said.

"I know."

"I'll do my best."

"Of course. And it will work. For good or ill, it will work."

"For good and ill, General. I hope so."

10

"Too much," said Jerry back in the pagoda, drinking tea from cracked Manchu bowls, eating shortbread from elegant polystyrene ware that had been smuggled from the factories at Shimabara or Kure.

The generals frowned. "Too much?"

"But the logic," said General Way Hahng, the most beautiful of the three.

"True," said Jerry, who was now in love with the generals and very much in love with General Way Hahng. For that general in particular he was prepared (temporarily or metatemporally, depending how it grabbed him) to compromise his principles, or at least not speak his mind fully. In a moment of self-exasperation he frowned. "False."

General Way Hahng's expression was disappointed. "But you said . . ."

"I meant 'true'," said Jerry. It was no good. But the sooner he was out of this one the better. Something had to give shortly. Or, at very least, someone. He suddenly remembered the great upsurge of enthusiasm among American painters immediately after the war and a Pollock came to mind. "Damn."

"It is a question of mathematics, of history," said the second general.

Jerry's breathing had become rapid.

11

"I do not read French," said General Way Hahng disdainfully handing the piece of paper back to Jerry. This was the first time they had been alone together.

Jerry sighed.

12

A shout.

13

As always it was a question of gestures. He remembered the way in which the wing of the F111A had drooped, hiding the ruin of the undercarriage. Whatever fallacy might exist – and perhaps one did – he was prepared to go along with it. After all, his admiration and enthusiasm had once been generous and it was the sort of thing you couldn't forget; there was always the sense of loss, no matter what you did to cover it up. Could he not continue to be generous, even though it was much more difficult? He shrugged. He had tried more than once and been rejected too often. A clean break was best.

But the impulse to make yet another gesture – of sympathy, of understanding, of love – was there. He knew no way in which such a gesture would not be safely free of misinterpretation, and he was, after all, the master forger. There was enormous substance there, perhaps more than ever before, but its expression was strangled. Why was he always ultimately considered the aggressor? Was it true? Even General Lee had seen him in that rôle. Chiefly, he supposed, it was as much as anything a question of equilibrium. Perhaps he simply had to reconcile himself to a long wait.

In the meantime, duty called, a worthy enough substitute for the big search. He stood on the top floor of the pagoda, forcing himself to confront the lake, which seemed to him as vast as the sea and very much deeper.

14

Memory made the martyr hurry; duality. Past was future. Memory was precognition. It was by no means a matter of matter. Karl Glogauer pinioned on a wooden cross by iron spikes through hands and feet.

"But if you would believe the unholy truth – then Time is an agony of Now, and so it will always be." – *The Dreaming City.* Do Not Analyse.

15

Devious notions ashamed the memory of his father's fake Le Corbusier château. But all that was over. It was a great relief.

"It is cool in here now," said General Way Hahng.

"You'd better come out," he said cautiously. "Quick. The eye. While it is open."

They stood together in the room and Jerry's love filled it.

"It is beautiful," said the General.

Weeping with pity, Jerry stroked the general's black hair, bent and kissed the lips. "Soon." The vibragun and the rest of the equipment was handy.

16

A SWEET SHOUT.

17

The voice of the flatworm. Many-named, many-sided, meta-temporal operative extraordinary, man of the multiverse, meta-physician metahealed metaselfed. The acid voice.

" 'God,' said Renark and he lived that moment forever." – *The Sundered Worlds*

18

The flow of the Mandarin, the quality of the Sanskrit that the general spoke in love. It all made sense. Soon. But let the victim call once more, move once more.

19

Jerry went to the window, looked out at the lake, at the black and shining water.

Behind him in the room General Way Hahng lay naked, smoking a powerful dose. The general's eyes were hooded and the general's lips curved in a beatific, almost stupid, smile. The little visitaper by the side of the mattress cast abstract images on the mosaic of the wall, played *What You're Doing*, but even that made Jerry impatient. At this moment he rarely wanted complete silence, but now he must have it. He strolled across the room and waved the visitaper into silence. He had the right. The general did not dispute it.

Jerry glanced at his discarded outfit and touched his clean chin. Had he gone too far?

His own heavy intake was making his heart thump as if in passion. There had been his recent meeting with the poet he admired but who denied himself too much. "Irony is often a substitute for real imagination," the poet had said, speaking about a recent interplanetary extravaganza.

But all that was a distraction now. It was time.

Jerry bowed his head before the lake. Sentiment, not the water, had overcome him momentarily. Did it matter?

20

Jerry pointed the vibragun at the general and watched the body shake for several minutes. Then he took the extractor and applied it. Soon the infinitely precious nucleotides were stored and he prepared to leave. He kissed the corpse swiftly, put the box that was now the general under his arm. In Washington there was a chef who would know what to do.

He climbed down through the floors to where the remaining generals were waiting for him.

"Tell General Lee the operation was conducted," he said.

"How will you leave?"

"I have transportation" said Jerry.

21

The lovebeast left China the next morning carrying Jerry Cornelius with it, either as a rider or against his will: those who saw them pass found it impossible to decide. Perhaps even Jerry or the beast itself no longer knew, they had moved about the world together for so long.

Like a dragon it rose into the wind, heading for the ruined, the rich and rolling lands of the west.

The Delhi Division

1

A smoky Indian rain fell through the hills and woods outside Simla and the high roads were slippery. Jerry Cornelius drove his Phantom V down twisting lanes flanked by white fences. The car's violet body was splashed with mud and it was difficult to see through the haze that softened the landscape. In rain, the world became timeless.

Jerry switched on his music, singing along with Jimi Hendrix as he swung around the corners.

Were they finding the stuff? He laughed involuntarily.

Turning into the drive outside his big wooden bungalow, he

brought the limousine to a stop. A Sikh servant gave him an umbrella before taking over the car.

Jerry walked through the rain to the veranda; folding the umbrella he listened to the sound of the water on the leaves of the trees, like the ticking of a thousand watches.

He had come home to Simla and he was moved.

2

In the hut was a small neatly made bed and on the bed an old toy bear. Above it a blown-up picture of Alan Powys had faded in the sun. A word had been scratched into the wall below and to the left of the picture:

ASTRAPHOBIA

By the side of the bed was a copy of *Vogue* for 1952, a *Captain Marvel* comic book, a clock in a square case. The veneer of the clock case had been badly burned. Propping up the clock at one corner was an empty Pall Mall pack which had faded to a pinkish colour and was barely recognisable. Roaches crawled across the grey woollen blankets on the bed.

Rain rattled on the corrugated asbestos roof. Jerry shut and locked the door behind him. For the moment he could not concern himself with the hut. Perhaps it was just as well.

He looked through the waving trees at the ruined mansion. What was the exact difference between synthesis and sensationalism?

3

Jerry stayed in for the rest of the afternoon, oiling his needle rifle. Aggression sustained life, he thought. It had to be so; there were many simpler ways of procreating.

Was this why his son had died before he was born?

A servant brought in a silver tray containing a bottle of Pernod, some ice, a glass. Jerry smiled at it nostalgically, then broke the rifle in order to oil the barrel.

4

The ghost of his unborn son haunted him; though here, in the cool bungalow with its shadowed passages, it was much easier to bear. Of course, it had never been particularly hard to ignore; really a different process altogether. The division between imagination and spirit had not begun to manifest itself until quite late, at about the age of six or seven. Imagination – usually displayed at that age in quite ordinary childish games – had twice led him close to a lethal accident. In escaping, as always, he had almost run over a cliff.

Soon after that first manifestation the nightmares had begun, and then, coupled with the nightmares, the waking visions of twisted, malevolent faces, almost certainly given substance by *Fantasia*, his father's final treat before he had gone away.

Then the horrors increased as puberty came and he at last found a substitute for them in sexual fantasies of a grandiose and sado-masochistic nature. Dreams of jewelled elephants, cowed slaves and lavishly dressed rajahs parading through baroque streets while crowds of people in turbans and loincloths cheered them, jeered at them.

With some distaste Jerry stirred the fire in which burned the collection of religious books for children.

He was distracted by a sound from outside. On the veranda servants were shouting. He went to the window and opened it.

"What is it?"

"Nothing, sahib. A mongoose killing a cobra. See."

The man held up the limp body of the snake.

5

From the wardrobe Jerry took a coat of silk brocade. It was blue, with circles of a slightly lighter blue stitched into it with silver threads. The buttons were diamonds and the cloth was lined with buckram. The high, stiff collar was fixed at the throat by two hidden brass knuckles. Jerry put the coat on over his white silk shirt and trousers. Carefully he did up the buttons and then the collar. His long black hair fell over the shoulders of the coat and his rather dark features, with the imperial beard and moustache, fitted the outfit perfectly.

Crossing the bedroom, he picked up the rifle from the divan. He slotted on the telescopic sight, checked the magazine, cradled the gun in his left arm. A small drop of oil stained the silk.

Pausing by a chest of drawers he took an old-fashioned leather helmet and goggles from the top drawer.

He went outside and watched the ground steam in the sun. The ruined mansion was a bright, sharp white in the distance. Beyond it he could see his servants wheeling the light Tiger Moth biplane on to the small airfield.

6

A journey of return through the clear sky; a dream of flying; wheeling over blue-grey hills and fields of green rice, over villages and towns and winding yellow roads, over herds of cattle; over ancient, faded places, over rivers and hydro-electric plants; a dream of freedom.

In the distance, Delhi looked as graceful as New York.

7

Jerry made his way through the crowd of peons who had come to look at his plane. The late Victorian architecture of this suburb of Delhi blended in perfectly with the new buildings, including a Protestant church, which had been erected in the last ten years.

He pulled the flying goggles on to his forehead, shifted the gun from his left arm to his right and pushed open the doors of the church.

It was quite fancifully decorated, with murals in orange, blue and gold by local artists, showing incidents from the life of Jesus and the Apostles. The windows were narrow and unstained; the only other decoration was the altar and its furnishings. The pulpit was plain, of polished wood.

When Jerry was halfway down the aisle a young Indian priest appeared. He wore a buff-coloured linen suit and a dark blue shirt with a white dog-collar and he addressed Jerry in Hindi.

"We do not allow guns in the church, sir."

Jerry ignored him. "Where is Sabiha?"

The priest folded his hands on his stomach. "Sabiha is in Gandhinagar, I heard this morning. She left Ahmadabad yesterday. . . ."

"Is the Pakistani with her?"

"I should imagine so." The priest broke into English. "They have a tip-top car – a Rolls-Royce. It will get them there in no time."

Jerry smiled. "Good."

"You know Sabiha, then?" said the priest conversationally, beginning to walk towards Jerry.

Jerry levelled the needle rifle at his hip. "Of course. You don't recognise me?"

"Oh, my god!"

Jerry sighed and tilted the rifle a little. He pulled the trigger and sent a needle up through the priest's open mouth and into his brain.

In the long run, he supposed it was all a problem of equilibrium. But even considering his attitude towards the priest, the job was an unpleasant one. Naturally it would have been far worse if the priest had had an identity of his own. No great harm had been done, however, and on that score everybody would be more or less satisfied.

8

THERE are times in the history of a nation when random news events trickling from an unfriendly neighbour should be viewed not as stray birds but as symbols of a brood, the fingerposts of a frame of mind invested with sinister significance.

WHAT is precisely happening in Pakistan? Is there a gradual preparation, insidiously designed to establish dangerous tensions between the two neighbours?

WHY are the so-called Majahids being enrolled in large numbers and given guerrilla training? Why have military measures like the setting up of pill-boxes and similar offensive-defensive

steps on the border been escalated up to an alarming degree?
– *Blitz* news weekly, Bombay, 27 July 1968

9.

Through the half-constructed buildings of Gandhinagar Jerry
wandered, his flying helmet and goggles in one hand, his rifle in
the other. His silk coat was grubby now and open at the collar.
His white trousers were stained with oil and mud and his suede
boots were filthy. The Tiger Moth lay where he had crash-landed
it, one wheel completely broken off its axle. He wouldn't be able
to use it to leave.

It was close to sunset and the muddy streets were full of
shadows cast by the skeletons of modern skyscrapers on which
little work had been done for months. Jerry reached the tallest
building, one that had been planned as the government's chief administration block, and began to climb the ladders which had been
placed between the levels of scaffolding. He left his helmet behind,
but held the rifle by its trigger guard as he climbed.

When he reached the top and lay flat on the roofless concrete
wall he saw that the city seemed to have been planned as a spiral,
with this building as its axis. From somewhere on the outskirts of
the city a bell began to toll. Jerry pushed off the safety catch.

Out of a sidestreet moved a huge bull elephant with curling
tusks embellished with bracelets of gold, silver and bronze. On its
head and back were cloths of beautifully embroidered silk, weighted
with tassels of red, yellow and green; its howdah was also ornate,
the wood inlaid with strips of enamelled brass and silver, with onyx,
emeralds and sapphires. In the howdah lay Sabiha and the Pakistani,
their clothes disarrayed, making nervous love.

Jerry sighted down the gun's telescope until the back of the
Pakistani's head was in the cross hairs, but then the man moved as
Sabiha bit his shoulder and a strand of her blue nylon sari was
caught by the evening wind, floating up to obscure them both. When
the nylon drifted down again Jerry saw that they were both close
to orgasm. He put his rifle on the wall and watched. It was over
very quickly.

With a wistful smile he picked up his gun by the barrel and

dropped it over the wall so that it fell through the interior of the building, striking girders and making them ring like a glockenspiel.

The couple looked up but didn't see Jerry. Shortly afterwards the elephant moved out of sight.

Jerry began to climb slowly back down the scaffolding.

10

As he walked away from the city he saw the Majahid commandos closing in on the street where he supposed the elephant was. They wore crossed ammunition belts over their chests and carried big Lee-Enfield .303s. The Pakistani would be captured, doubtless, and Sabiha would have to find her own way back to Delhi. He took his spare keys from his trouser pocket and opened the door of the violet Rolls-Royce, climbed in and started the engine. He would have to stop for petrol in Ahmadabad, or perhaps Udaipur if he went that way.

He switched on the headlights and drove carefully until he came to the main highway.

11

In the bath he examined the scar on his inner thigh; he had slipped while getting over a corrugated iron fence cut to jagged spikes at the top so that people wouldn't climb it. He had been seven years old: fascinated at what the gash in his flesh revealed. For hours he had alternately bent and straightened his leg in order to watch the exposed muscles move through the seeping blood.

He got out of the bath and wrapped a robe around his body, walking slowly through the bungalow's passages until he reached his bedroom.

Sabiha had arrived. She gave him a wry smile. "Where's your gun?"

"I left it in Gandhinagar. I was just too late."

"I'm sorry."

He shrugged. "We'll be working together again, I hope."

"This scene's finished now, isn't it?"

"Our bit of it, anyway, I should think." He took a brass box from the dressing table and opened the lid, offering it to her. She looked into his eyes.

When she had taken all she needed, she closed the lid of the box with her long index finger. The sharp nails were painted a deep red.

Exhausted, Jerry fell back on the bed and stared at her vaguely as she changed out of her nylon sari into khaki drill trousers, shirt and sandals. She bunched up her long black hair and pinned it on top of her head.

"Your son . . ." she began, but Jerry closed his eyes, cutting her short.

He watched her turn and leave the room, then he switched out the light and very quickly went to sleep.

12

THE unbridled support given to the Naga rebels by China shows that India has to face alarums and excursions on both sides of her frontier. It is not likely that China would repeat her NEFA adventure of 1962, as she might then have to contend with the united opposition of the USSR and the USA.

THAT is precisely why the stellar role of a cat's paw appears to have been assigned to Pakistan. . . .

OUR Intelligence service should be kept alert so that we get authentic information well in advance of the enemy's intended moves.

AND once we receive Intelligence of any offensive being mounted, we should take the lesson from Israel to strike first and strike hard on several fronts before the enemy gets away withthe initial advantages of his blitzkrieg. – *Blitz*, ibid.

13

Waterfall by Jimi Hendrix was playing on the tape as Jerry ate his breakfast on the veranda. He watched a mongoose dart out from under the nearby hut and dash across the lawn towards the trees and the ruined mansion. It was a fine, cool morning.

As soon as the mongoose was safe, Jerry reached down from

the table and touched a stud on the floor. The hut disappeared. Jerry took a deep breath and felt much better. He hadn't accomplished everything, but his personal objectives had been tied up very satisfactorily. All that remained was for a woman to die. This had not, after all, been a particularly light-hearted episode.

14

KRISHNAN MOHAN JUNEJA (Ahmadabad): How you have chosen the name BLITZ and what does it mean?
It was started in 1941 at the height of Nazi blitzkrieg against Britain. — Blitz, ibid, correspondence column

15

At least there would be a little less promiscuous violence which was such a waste of everybody's life and time and which depressed him so much. If the tension had to be sustained, it could be sustained on as abstract a level as possible. And yet, did it finally matter at all? It was so hard to find that particular balance between law and chaos.

It was a dangerous game, a difficult decision, perhaps an irreconcilable dichotomy.

16

As he walked through the trees towards the ruined mansion he decided that in this part of the world things were narrowing down too much. He wished that he had not missed his timing where the Pakistani was concerned. If he had killed him, it might have set in motion a whole new series of cross-currents. He had slipped up and he knew why.

The mansion's roof had fallen in and part of the front wall bulged outwards. All the windows were smashed in the lower storeys and the double doors had been broken backwards on their hinges. Had he the courage to enter? The presence of his son was very strong.

If only it had not been here, he thought. Anywhere else and the Pakistani would be dead by now.

Until this moment he had never considered himself to be a coward, but he stopped before he got to the doorway and could not move forward. He wheeled round and began to run, his face moving in terror.

The Phantom V was ready. He got into it and drove it rapidly down the drive and out into the road. He went away from Simla and he was screaming, his eyes wide with self-hatred. His scream grew louder as he passed Delhi and it only died completely when he reached Bombay and the coast.

He was weeping uncontrollably even when the SS *Kao An* was well out into the Arabian Sea.

The Tank Trapeze

01.00 hours:

Prague Radio announced the move and said the Praesidium of the Czechoslovak Communist Party regarded it as a violation of international law, and that Czechoslovak forces had been ordered not to resist.

*   *   *

Perfection had always been his goal, but a sense of justice had usually hampered him. Jerry Cornelius wouldn't be seeing the burning city again. His only luggage an expensive cricket bag, he rode a scheduled corpse boat to the Dubrovnik depot and boarded the SS *Kao An* bound for Burma, arriving just in time.

After the ship had jostled through the junks to find a berth, Jerry disembarked, making his way to the Rangoon public baths where, in a three kyat cubicle, he took off his brown serge suit and turban, changing into an elaborately embroidered Russian blouse loose enough to hide his shoulder holster. From his bag he took a pair of white flannels, soft Arabian boots and an old-fashioned astrakhan shako. Disguised to his satisfaction he left the baths and went by pedicab to the checkpoint where the Buddhist monk waited for him.

The monk's moody face was fringed by a black "Bergman" beard making him look like an unfrocked BBC producer. Signing the safe-conduct order with a Pentel pen that had been recharged in some local ink, he blinked at Jerry. "He's here today."

"Too bad." Jerry adjusted his shako with the tips of his fingers then gave the monk his heater. The monk shrugged, looked at it curiously and handed it back. "Okay. Come on. There's a car."

"*Every gun makes its own tune,*" murmured Jerry.

As they headed for the old Bentley tourer parked beyond the guard hut, the monk's woolly saffron cardigan billowed in the breeze.

*　　　*　　　*

02.15

All telephone lines between Vienna and Czechoslovakia were cut.

*　　　*　　　*

They drove between the green paddy fields and in the distance saw the walls of Mandalay. Jerry rubbed his face. "I hadn't expected it to be so hot."

"Hell, isn't it? It'll be cooler in the temple." The monk's eyes were on the twisting white road.

Jerry wound down the window. Dust spotted his blouse but he didn't bother to brush it off. "Lai's waiting in the temple, is he?"

The monk nodded. "Is that what you call him? Could you kill a child, Mr Cornelius?"

"I could try."

*   *   *

03.45

Prague Radio and some of its transmitters were off the air.

*   *   *

All the roofs of Mandalay were of gold or burnished brass. Jerry put on his dark glasses as they drove through the glazed gates. The architecture was almost primitive and somewhat fierce. Hindu rather than Buddhist in inspiration, it featured as decoration a variety of boldly painted devils, fabulous beasts and minor deities.

"You keep it up nicely."

"We do our best. Most of the buildings, of course, are in the later Pala-Sena style."

"The spires in particular."

"Wait till you see the temple."

The temple was rather like an Anuradhapuran ziggurat, rising in twelve ornate tiers of enamelled metal inlaid with silver, bronze, gold, onyx, ebony and semi-precious stones. Its entrance was overhung by three arches, each like an inverted V, one upon the other. The building seemed overburdened, like a tree weighted with too much ripe fruit. They went inside, making their way between pillars of carved ivory and teak. Of the gods in the carvings, Ganesh was the one most frequently featured.

"The expense, of course, is enormous," whispered the monk. "Here's where we turn off."

A little light entered the area occupied chiefly by a reclining Buddha of pure gold, resting on a green marble plinth. The Buddha was twenty feet long and about ten feet high, a decadent copy in the manner of the Siamese school of U Thong. The statue's thick lips were supposed to be curved in a smile but instead seemed fatuously pursed.

From the shadow of the Buddha a man moved into the light.

He was fat, the colour of oil, with a crimson fez perched on his bald head. His hands were buried in the pockets of his beige jacket. "You're Jeremiah Cornelius? You're pale. Haven't been out east long . . ."

"This is Captain Maxwell," said the monk eagerly.

"I was to meet a Mr Lai."

"This is Mr Lai."

"How do you do." Jerry put down his cricket bag.

"How do you do, Mr Cornelius."

"It depends what you mean."

Captain Maxwell pressed his lips in a red smile. "I find your manner instructive." He waved the monk away and returned to the shadows. "Will it matter, I wonder, if we are not simpatico?"

*　　　*　　　*

03.30

Russian troops took up positions outside the Prague Radio building.

*　　　*　　　*

In the bamboo bar of the Mandalay Statler-Hilton Jerry looked through the net curtains at the rickshaws passing rapidly on both sides of the wide street. The bar was faded and poorly stocked and its only other occupants, two German railway technicians on their way through to Laos, crossed the room to the far corner and began a game of bar billiards.

Jerry took the stool next to Captain Maxwell who had registered at the same time, giving his religion as Protestant and his occupation as engineer. Jerry asked the Malayan barman for a Jack Daniels that cost him fourteen kyats and tasted like clock oil.

"This place doesn't change," Maxwell said. His Slavic face was morose as he sipped his sherbet. "I don't know why I come back. Nowhere else, I suppose. Came here first . . ." He rubbed his toothbrush moustache with his finger and used the same finger to push a ridge of sweat from his forehead. Fidgeting for a moment on his stool he dismounted to tug at the material that had stuck to the sweat of his backside. "Don't touch the curries here. They're murder. The other grub's okay though. A bit dull." He picked up his glass and was surprised to find it empty. "You flew in, did you?"

"Boat in. Flying out."

Maxwell rolled his sleeves up over his heavy arms and slapped at a mosquito that had settled among the black hairs and the pink, torn bites. "God almighty. Looking for women?"

Jerry shrugged.

"They're down the street. You can't miss the place."

"See you." Jerry left the bar. He got into a taxi and gave an address in the suburbs beyond the wall.

As they moved slowly through the teeming streets the taxi driver leaned back and studied Jerry's thin face and long blond hair. "Boring now, sir. Worse than the Japs now, sir."

*   *   *

03.45

Soviet tanks and armoured cars surrounded the party Central Committee's building in Prague.

*   *   *

From the other side of the apartment's oak door Jerry heard the radio, badly tuned to some foreign station, playing the younger Dvořák's lugubrious piano piece, *The Railway Station at Cierna nad Tisov*. He rang the bell. Somebody changed the channel and the radio began to play *Alexander's Ragtime Band*, obviously performed by one of the many Russian traditional jazz bands that had become so popular in recent years. A small woman in a blue cheong sam, her black hair piled on her head, opened the door and stepped demurely back to let him in. He winked at her.

"You're Anna Ne Win?"

She bowed her head and smiled.

"You're something."

"And so are you."

On the heavy chest in the hallway stood a large Ming vase of crimson roses.

The rest of the apartment was full of the heavy scent of carnations. It was a little overpowering.

*　　　*　　　*

03.47

Prague Radio went off the air completely.

*　　　*　　　*

The child's body was covered from throat to ankles by a gown on to which intricately cut jewels had been stitched so that none of the material showed through. On his shaven head was a similarly worked cap. His skin was a light, soft brown and he seemed a sturdy little boy, grave and good looking. When Jerry entered the gloomy, scented room, the child let out a huge sigh, as if he had been holding his breath for several minutes. His hands emerged from his long sleeves and he placed one on each arm of the ornate wooden chair over which his legs dangled. "Please sit down."

Jerry took off his shako and looked carefully into the boy's large almond eyes before lowering himself to the cushion near the base of the chair.

"You've seen Lai?"

Jerry grinned. "You could be twins."

The boy smiled and relaxed in the chair. "Do you like children, Mr Cornelius?"

"I try to like whatever's going."

"Children like me. I am different, you see." The boy unbuttoned his coat, exposing his downy brown chest. "Reach up, Mr Cornelius, and put your hand on my heart."

Jerry leaned forward and stretched out his hand. He placed his palm against the child's smooth chest. The beat was rapid and irregular. Again he looked into the child's eyes and was interested by the ambiguities he saw in them. For a moment he was afraid.

"Can I see your gun, Mr Cornelius?"

Jerry took his hand away and reached under his blouse, tugging his heater from his holster. He gave it to the child who drew it up close to his face to inspect it. "I have never seen a gun like this before."

"It's a side-product," Jerry said, retrieving the weapon, "of the communications industry."

"Ah, of course. What do you think will happen?"

"Who knows? We live in hope."

Anna Ne Win, dressed in beautiful brocade, with her hair hanging free, returned with a tray, picking her way among the cushions that were scattered everywhere on the floor of the gloomy room. "Here is some tea. I hope you'll dally with us."

"I'd love to."

*   *   *

04.20

The Soviet Tass Agency said that Soviet troops had been called into Czechoslovakia by Czechoslovak leaders.

*   *   *

In the hotel room Maxwell picked his nails with a splintered chopstick while Jerry checked his kit.

"You'll be playing for the visitors, of course. Hope the weather won't get you down."

"It's got to get hotter before it gets cooler."

"What do you mean by that?" Maxwell lit a Corona from the butt of a native cheroot he had just dropped in the ashtray, watching Jerry undo the straps of his bag.

Jerry up-ended the cricket bag. All the equipment tumbled noisily on to the bamboo table and hit the floor. A red cricket ball rolled under the bed. Maxwell was momentarily disconcerted, then leaned down and recovered it. His chair creaked as he tossed the ball to Jerry.

Jerry put the ball in his bag and picked up a protector and a pair of bails. "The smell of brand-new cricket gear. Lovely, isn't it?"

"I've never played cricket."

Jerry laughed. "Neither have I. Not since I had my teeth knocked out when I was five."

"You're considering violence, then?"

"I don't get you."

"What is it you dislike about me?"

"I hadn't noticed. Maybe I'm jealous."

"That's quite likely."

"I've been aboard your yacht, you see. The *Teddy Bear*. In the Pool of London. Registered in Hamburg, isn't she?"

"The *Teddy Bear* isn't my yacht, Mr Cornelius. If only she were. Is that all . . . ?"

"Then it must be Tsarapkin's, eh?"

"You came to Mandalay to do a job for me, Mr Cornelius, not to discuss the price of flying fish."

Jerry shrugged. "You raised the matter."

"That's rich."

*   *   *

04.45

Prague radio came back on the air and urged the people of Prague to heed only the legal voice of Czechoslovakia. It repeated the request not to resist. "We are incapable of defending these frontiers," it said.

*   *   *

Caught at the wicket for sixteen off U Shi Jheon, Jerry now sat in his deckchair watching the game. Things looked sticky for the visitors.

It was the first few months of 1948 that had been crucial. A detailed almanac for that period would reveal a lot. That was when the psychosis had really started to manifest itself. It had been intensifying ever since. There was only a certain amount one could do, after all.

*   *   *

06.25

Russian troops began shooting at Czechoslovak demonstrators outside the Prague Radio building.

*   *   *

While Jerry was changing, Captain Maxwell entered the dressing room and stood leaning against a metal locker, rubbing his right foot against his fat left leg while Jerry combed his hair.

"How did the match go?"

"A draw. What did you expect?"

"No less."

"You didn't do too badly out there, old boy. Tough luck, being caught like that."

Jerry blew him a kiss and left the pavilion, carrying his cricket bag across the empty field towards the waiting car that could just be seen through the trees.

* * *

06.30

Machine-gun fire broke out near the Hotel Esplanade.

* * *

Jerry strolled among the pagodas as the sun rose and struck their bright roofs. Shaven-headed monks in saffron moved slowly here and there. Jerry's boots made no sound on the mosaic paths. Looking back, he saw that Anna Ne Win was watching him from the corner of a pagoda. At that moment the child appeared and took her hand, leading her out of sight. Jerry walked on.

* * *

06.30

Prague television was occupied.

* * *

Maxwell stared down through the window, trying to smooth the wrinkles in his suit. "Rangoon contacted me last night."

"Ah."

"They said: 'It is better to go out in the street.'" Maxwell removed his fez. "It's all a matter of profits in the long run, I suppose." He chuckled.

"You seem better this morning. The news must have been good."

"Positive. You could call it positive. I must admit I was beginning to get a little nervy. I'm a man of action, you see, like yourself."

* * *

06.37

Czech National Anthem played.

* * *

Anna Ne Win moved her soft body against his in the narrow bed, pushing his legs apart with her knee. Raising himself on one elbow he reached out and brushed her black hair from her face. It was almost afternoon. Her delicate eyes opened and she smiled.

He turned away.

"Are you crying, Jerry?"

Peering through the slit in the blind he saw a squadron of L-29 Delfins fly shrieking over the golden rooftops. Were they part of an occupation force? He couldn't make out the markings. For a moment he felt depressed, then he cheered up, anticipating a pleasant event.

* * *

06.36

Prague Radio announced: "When you hear the Czech National Anthem you will know it's all over."

* * *

Jerry hung around the post office the whole day. No reply came to his telegram but that was probably a good sign. He went to a bar in the older part of the city where a Swedish folk-singer drove him out. He took a rickshaw ride around the wall. He bought a necklace and a comb. In Ba Swe Street he was almost hit by a racing tram and while he leaned against a telephone pole two *Kalan cacsa* security policemen made him show them his safe conduct. It impressed them. He watched them saunter through the crowd on the pavement and arrest a shoeshine boy, pushing him aboard the truck which had been crawling behind them. A cathartic act, if not a kindly one.

Jerry found himself in a deserted street. He picked up the brushes and rags and the polish. He fitted them into the box and placed it neatly in a doorway. A few people began to reappear. A tram came down the street. On the opposite pavement, Jerry saw Captain Maxwell. The engineer stared at him suspiciously until he realised Jerry had seen him, then he waved cheerfully. Jerry pretended he hadn't noticed and withdrew into the shade of a tattered awning. The shop itself, like so many in the street, had been closed for some time and its door and shutters were fastened by heavy iron padlocks. A proclamation had been pasted on one door panel. Jerry made out the words *Pyee-Daung-Su Myanma-Nainggan-Daw*. It was an official notice, then. Jerry watched the rickshaws and cars, the trams and the occasional truck pass in the street.

After a while the shoeshine boy returned. Jerry pointed out his equipment. The boy picked it up and walked with it under his arm towards the square where the Statler-Hilton could be seen. Jerry decided he might as well follow him, but the boy began to run and turned hastily into a side street.

Jerry spat into the gutter.

*　　　*　　　*

07.00

President Svoboda made a personal appeal over the radio for calm. He said he could offer no explanation for the invasion.

*　　　*　　　*

As Jerry checked the heater's transistors, Maxwell lay on the unmade bed watching him. "Have you any other occupation, Mr Cornelius?"

"I do this and that."

"And what about political persuasions?"

"There you have me, Captain Maxwell."

"Our monk told me you said it was as primitive to hold political convictions as it was to maintain belief in God." Maxwell loosened his cummerbund.

"Is that a fact?"

"Or was he putting words into your mouth?"

Jerry clipped the heater back together. "It's a possibility."

*   *   *

08.20

Pilsen Radio described itself as "the last free radio station in Czechoslovakia".

*   *   *

A Kamov Ka-15 helicopter was waiting for them on the cricket field near the pavilion. Maxwell offered the pilot seat to Jerry. They clambered in and adjusted their flying helmets.

"You've flown these before," said Maxwell.

"That's right." Jerry lit a cheroot.

"*The gestures of conflict keep the peace*," murmured Maxwell nostalgically.

*   *   *

10.00

The Czechoslovak agency Četeka said that at least ten ambulances had arrived outside Prague Radio station, where a Soviet tank was on fire.

*   *   *

When they had crossed the Irrawaddy, Jerry entered the forest and headed for the shrine. He had a map in one hand and a compass in the other.

The atmosphere of the forest was moist and cool. It would

begin to rain soon; already the sky was becoming overcast. The air was full of little clusters of flies and mosquitoes, like star systems encircling an invisible sun, and in avoiding them Jerry knocked off his shako several times. His boots were now muddy and his blouse and trousers stained by the bark and foliage. He stumbled on.

About an hour later the birches began to thin out and he knew he was close to the clearing. He breathed heavily, moving more cautiously.

He saw the chipped green tiles of the roof first, then the dirty ivory columns that supported it, then the shrine itself. Under the roof, on a base of rusting steel sheeting, stood a fat Buddha carved from local stone and painted in dark reds, yellows and blues. The statue smiled. Jerry crawled through the damp undergrowth until he could get a good view of the boy.

A few drops of rain fell loudly on the roof. Already the ground surrounding the shrine was churned to mud by a previous rainfall. The boy lay in the mud, face down, arms flung out towards the shrine, legs stiffly together, his jewelled gown covering his body. One ankle was just visible; the brown flesh showing in the gap between the slipper and the hem. Jerry touched his lips with the tip of his finger.

Above his head monkeys flung themselves through the green branches as they looked for cover from the rain. The noise they made helped Jerry creep into the clearing unobserved. He frowned.

The boy lifted his head and smiled up at Jerry. "Do you feel like a woman?"

"You stick to your prayers, I'll stick to mine."

The boy obeyed. Jerry stood looking down at the little figure as it murmured the prayers. He took out his heater and cleared his throat, then he adjusted the beam width and burned a thin hole through the child's anus. He screamed.

Later Maxwell emerged from the undergrowth and began removing the various quarters from the jewelled material. There was hardly any blood, just the stench. He shook out the bits of flesh and folded the parts of the gown across his arm. He put one slipper in his right pocket and the other in his left. Lastly he plucked the cap from the severed head and offered it to Jerry.

"You'd better hurry. The rain's getting worse. We'll be

drowned at this rate. That should cover your expenses. You'll be able to convert it fairly easily in Singapore."

"I don't often get expenses," said Jerry.

*　　*　*

10.25

Četeka said shooting in the centre of Prague had intensified and that the "Rude Pravo" offices had been seized by "occupation units".

*　　*　　*

Waiting near the Irrawaddy for the Ka-15 to come back, Jerry watched the rain splash into the river. He was already soaked.

The flying field had only recently been cleared from the jungle and it went right down to the banks of the river. Jerry picked his teeth with his thumbnail and looked at the broad brown water and the forest on the other side. A wooden landing stage had been built out into the river and a family of fishermen were tying up their sampan. Why should crossing this particular river seem so important?

Jerry shook his umbrella and looked up at the sound of the helicopter's engines. He was completely drenched; he felt cold and he felt sorry for himself. The sooner he could reach the Galapagos the better.

*　　*　　*

11.50

Pilsen Radio said: "The occupation has already cost twenty-five lives."

*　　*　　*

He just got to the post office before it closed. Anna Ne Win was standing inside reading a copy of *Dandy*. She looked up. "You're British, aren't you? Want to hear the Test results?"

Jerry shook his head. It was pointless asking for his telegram now. He no longer had any use for assurances. What he needed most at this stage was a good, solid, undeniable fact; something to get his teeth into.

"A Captain Maxwell was in earlier for some money that was being cabled to him," she said. "Apparently he was disappointed. Have you found it yet – the belt?"

"I'm sorry, no."

"You should have watched where you threw it."

"Yes."

"That Captain Maxwell. He's staying at your hotel, isn't he?"

"Yes. I've got to leave now. Going to Singapore. I'll buy you two new ones there. Send them along." He ran from the post office.

"Cheerio," she called. "Keep smiling."

*　　　*　　　*

12.28

Četeka said Mr Dubček was under restriction in the Central Committee building.

*　　　*　　　*

Naked, Jerry sat down on his bed and smoked a cheroot. He was fed up with the east. It wasn't doing his identity any good.

The door opened and Maxwell came in with a revolver in his hand and a look of disgust on his fat face. "You're not wearing any damned clothes!"

"I wasn't expecting you."

Maxwell cocked the revolver. "Who do you think you are, anyway?"

"Who do you think?"

Maxwell sneered. "You'd welcome suggestions, eh? I want to puke when I look at you."

"Couldn't I help you get a transfer?"

"I don't need one."

Jerry looked at the disordered bed, at the laddered stockings

Anna Ne Win had left behind, at the trousers hanging on the string over the washbasin, at the woollen mat on the floor by the bed, at the cricket bat on top of the wardrobe. "It would make me feel better, though." He drew on his cheroot. "Do you want the hat back?"

"Don't be revolting, Cornelius."

"What do you want, then, Captain Maxwell?"

"Justice."

"I'm with you." Jerry stood up and reached for his flannels. Maxwell raised the Webley and Scott .45 and fired the first bullet. Jerry was thrust against the washbasin and he blinked rapidly as his vision dimmed. There was a bruise five inches in diameter on his right breast and its centre was a hole with red, puckered sides; around the edges of the bruise a little blood was beginning to force its way out. "There certainly are some shits in the world," he said.

A couple of shots later, when Jerry was lying on the floor, he had the impression that Maxwell's trousers had fallen down. He grinned. Maxwell's voice was faint but insulting. "Bloody gangster! Murderer! Fucking killer!"

Jerry turned on his side and noticed that Anna Ne Win's cerise suspender belt was hanging on a spring under the bed. He reached out and touched it and a tremor of pleasure ran through his body. The last shot he felt hit the base of his spine.

He shuddered and was vaguely aware of the weight of Maxwell's lumpen body on his, of the insect-bitten wrists, of the warm Webley and Scott still in one hand and the cordite smell on the captain's breath. Then Maxwell whispered something in his ear and reaching around his face carefully folded down his eyelids.

(All quotes from the *Guardian*, 22 August 1968)

The Nature
of the Catastrophe

Introduction

The One Part Actress

Miss Brunner was firm about it. With her lips pursed she stood in the school's dark doorway. She knew she had him over a barrel.

Pretending to ignore her, Jerry Cornelius leafed through the tattered copy of *Business Week*. "The future that rides on Apollo 12 . . . Hunt for cancer vaccine closes in . . . What delayed the jumbo jets? . . . New sales pitch for disposables . . ."

Miss Brunner moved fast. She snatched the magazine from his hands.

"Look at me," she said. "Look at me."

He looked at her. "I'll be too many people by 1980. By 1980 I'll be dead." he said.

Her nostrils flared. "You've got to go."

His legs trembled. "It'll be murder."

She smiled. "It'll be murder," she said, "if you don't. Won't it?"

Jerry frowned. "It had to come. Sooner or later."

"It'll clear the air."

"What fucking air?" He gave her a hurt look. "Then?"

"Get busy, eh. You've got fifty years to play about in, after all."

"Fuck you!"

"And we'll have no more of that."

In the gym a wind-up gramophone played *Bye, Bye, Blackbird*.

Le Fratricide de la rue Clary

Genes began to pop.

Scenes fractured.

Jerry screamed.

They took his bicycle away. It was a gent's black roadster: "The Royal Albert". He had kept it up nicely.

"Hang on tight, Mr Cornelius."

"I'll bloody go where I . . ."

"This is it!"

The seedy street in Marseilles disappeared.

He didn't mind that.

In the Net

There was a drum beating somewhere and he could bet he knew who was beating it. Of all the superstitious notions he had encountered, the notion of "the future" was the most ludicrous. He was really lumbered now.

Development

The nerve gas plant at Portreath, Cornwall, is a pilot establishment for the Ministry of Defence, which has been manufacturing small quantities of gas for some time. Mrs Compton said the widow of one victim had not been allowed to see the pathologist's report or any other medical papers on her husband. – *Guardian*, 21 November 1969

Fantasy Review

After the gas attack Jerry Cornelius finished the washing-up and went out into the street. A rainbow had formed over Ladbroke Grove. Everything was very still. He bent to put on his bicycle clips.

"Jerry!"

"Yes, Mum?"

"You come back and dry up properly, you little bugger!"

The Impatient Dreamers

5 June 1928: Fifty-two years since Owen Nares and Jeanne de Casalis opened in Karen Bramson's *The Man They Buried* at the Ambassadors Theatre, London. The *Daily News* had said: ". . . at the end of all the tumult of life is 'Time and the unresolved hypothesis' ".

People Like You

Jerry groped his way from the car and turned his sightless eyes upward. Sunlight would not register. He was completely blind.

So it hadn't paid off.

Tears began to cruise down his cheeks.

"Mum?"

Somewhere in the distance the chatter of the Graf Zeppelin's engines died away.

He was abandoned.

Am I blue? You'd be too. If each plan with your man done fell through. Watcha gonna do? Watcha gonna do?

World to Conquer

We regret to say that Prince Jewan Bukht, son of the late Shah Bahudur Sha, the last titular King of Delhi, is dangerously ill . . . He is the last of his race that was born in the purple. He leaves a son, also in bad health, who was born in Rangoon while his father was in confinement. With Prince Jewan Bukht passes away the last direct descendant of the once famous house of Timour. – *Rangoon Times*, 28 July 1884

He struggled out of that.

Number 7

Jerry stumbled and fell, gashing his knee. He felt about him with his stone cold hands. He touched something as smooth as steel. He stroked the surfaces. A discarded suit of armour? And yet everywhere now were sounds. Engines. Screams.

Didn't he know there was a war on? Was he making it back?
He heard a bus draw up nearby, its motor turning over.
He shouted.
There was silence again. A V1 silence.
Coming in on a wing and a prayer . . .

The Ill Wind

The rush of water.
He was grasping at anything now.
He should never have tried it. A certain amount of diffusion could have been anticipated, but nothing as terrifying as this. He'd been conned.
Distantly: *One o'clock, two o'clock, three o'clock rock* . . .

The Adapters

There were strong sexual overtones which only became apparent as he concentrated, speaking aloud into the thinning air:

"Miss Jeanne de Casalis, who is the subject this week for our 'Is the Child Mother to the Woman?' series . . ."

"My father, who came from le pays Basque, had gone to Basutoland for the purpose of scientific investigations in connection with cancer and probable cures for this terrible disease, when a baby was announced . . ."

"Once the best and most popular fellow at Greyfriars – now the worst boy in the school! Such is the unhappy pass to which Harry Wharton's feud with his form-master leads him! You cannot ..."

"Issued July 15, 1931, to be used to prepay postage on mail carried aboard the Graf Zeppelin on its prospective flight to the North Pole. It was on this voyage that the *Nautilus*, a submarine commanded by Sir Hubert Wilkins, was to meet the Graf Zeppelin and transfer mail from one ship to the other at the North Pole. The *Nautilus* did not keep the rendezvous."

"Long Service Certificate. Presented by the Board of Directors to Ernest Frederick Cornelius of the W.D. & H.O. Wills Branch of the Imperial Tobacco Company (of Great Britain and Ireland), Limited, in Recognition of Faithful Service Rendered During the Past 25 Years and as a mark of Appreciation and Goodwill. Signed on behalf of the Board, Date 28th March 1929. Gilbert A. H. Wills, Chairman."

"Georges Duhamel, who has discovered a serum for cancer, is suddenly stricken with pain. He lives for the rest of the play in dread expectation of death. His whole nature changes ... (He) will not face an operation because that will proclaim to the world that his serum is a failure."

Jerry closed the scrapbook and opened the stamp album. It contained hundreds of Zeppelin issues from Paraguay. Liechtenstein, Latvia, Italy, Iceland, Greece, Germany, Cyrenaica, Cuba, Canada, Brazil, the Argentine, the Aegean Islands, the United States of America, San Marino, Russia. There were also a couple of Spanish autogiro issues and an Italian issue showing Leonardo da Vinci's flying machine.

From the little linen envelope beside the album, Jerry took with his tweezers his latest discovery, a set of Salvador airmail stamps issued on 15 September 1930. The stamps had become so brittle that they would split unless handled with great care. They were deep red (15c), emerald green (20c), brown violet (25c), ultramarine (40c) and all showed a biplane flying over San Salvador. This issue had just preceded the Simon Bolivar airmail issue of 17 December 1930.

"Jerry! You get down outa there an' 'elp yer mum!"
Jerry was oscillating badly.

The Merit Award

Jerry wandered over the bomb-site, kicking at bits of broken brick. The catharsis had come at last, then. But wasn't it a trifle disappointing?

Now he could go for miles and nothing would interrupt him.

Taking an apple from his pocket, he bit it, then spat, flinging the thing away. It had tasted of detergent.

He looked down at his hands. They were red and grey and they shook. He sat on a slab of broken concrete. Nothing moved. Nothing sang.

Shapers of Men

Changes in jewellery design styles tend to take place over a period of many years. In the past one could think in terms of millennia, centuries or generations, at the very least. Not so today. – Brian Marshall, *Illustrated London News*, 22 November 1969

Coming Next Issue

Jerry wondered why the scene had got so hazy. A few buildings stood out sharply, but everything else was drowned in mist. He put the Phantom X into reverse.

He wished they'd let him keep his bike.

How little time you were allowed for yourself. Twenty-five years at most. The rest belonged to and was manipulated by the ghosts of the past, the ghosts of the future. A generation was a hundred and fifty years. There was no escape.

A rocket roared by.

When the red, red robin comes bob, bob, bobbin' . . .

Prisoner in the Ice

By 1979, industrial technology will make the sixties seem like the dark ages. Automatic highways – computerised kitchens – person-to-person television – food from under the sea. They are ideas today, but industrial technology will make them a part of your life tomorrow ... Our measuring devices are so accurate they're used by the US Bureau of Standards to measure other measuring devices. Our fasteners were selected for the space suits on the men who walked the moon. Our plastic parts are in almost every automobile made in the USA.

In these ways, and more, we help make today's ideas tomorrow's realities. – US Industries Inc., ad., *New York Times*, 16 October 1969

"The waterline length is 1,004 ft., and when completed her tonnage will probably exceed 73,000. The *Queen Mary*'s maiden voyage (from Southampton to New York) begins on 27 May 1936 ..."

"Britain's toy soldiers have been ..."

"By 1980 there will be ..."

His voice was hoarse now. Fifty years was too long. He had no one, and no one to blame but himself.

Little man you're crying: I know why you're blue ...

Lucifer!

A hundred and fifty years itched in his skull and yet he could not get back to the only year in which he could survive.

From time to time his sight would return, allowing him horrifying visions – fragments of newspapers, buildings, roadways, cars, planes, skulls, ruins, ruins, ruins.

"MUM!"

"DAD!"

(CRASHED CONCORDE HAD RECEIVED FULL OVERHAUL)

"CATHY!"

"FRANK!"

(MARS MEN BACK IN DOCK)

"GRANDMA!"

"GRANDPA!"
(CHINESE MAKE FRESH GAINS)
"JERRY!"
(METS DO IT AGAIN — TEN IN A ROW!)
"Je..."

His voice whispered into near vacuum.

If only he had been allowed to bring his "Royal Albert" bike. It would have seen him through. It would have been an anchor.

But he was alone.

"M..."

Rootless, he was dying.

The cold was absolute. His body fell away from him.

The resurrection, if it came, would be painful.

Conclusion

A Man of Qualities

"That's a boy!"

"That's what you say." Jerry had had enough of it all. He shivered.

They unstrapped him from the chair. "Don't you feel better now?"

Jerry glanced around the Time Centre. All the chronographs were going like clockwork. "I told you it didn't exist," he said, "because I don't exist. Not there."

"It was worth a try, though, wasn't it?"

Jerry bunched himself up and tried to stop shaking.

A Kind and Thoughtful Friend

"It boils down to a question of character, doesn't it?" Miss Brunner said. "Character. Character."

She always knew how to get to him. She always chose a moment when his energy was at a low ebb.

He looked miserably up from the desk, hoping to touch her heart.

She knew he was confused. "And if I told your mother . . ."

He lowered his head again. Maybe it would all blow over.

It's a Beautiful, Glamorous Age

It had all gone now, of course. He'd used up the last of it. No more past to draw on. He felt at his skin.

"Smooth," he said.

"You see." She held her thin body in an attitude of triumph. "It was all for the best."

Other texts used:
The Sketch, 13 January 1926
The Bystander, 5 October 1927
T.P.'s Weekly, 26 November 1927
Daily Mail, 15 December 1927
Le Petit Marseillais, 22 October 1930
The Story of Navigation, Card No. 50, published by
The Imperial Tobacco Co., 1935
Standard Catalogue of Air Post Stamps, Sanabria,
New York, 1937
Modern Boy, 9 July 1938
Vision of Tomorrow, November 1939
The Illustrated Weekly of India, 6 July 1969

The Swastika Set-Up

Introduction

Often Dr Cornelius has said he should not interfere with the
calendar, for he almost invariably removes two sheets at the
same time and so produces even more confusion. The young
Xaver, however, apparently delights in this pastime and refuses
to be denied his pleasure. – Thomas Mann, *Disorder and Early
Sorrow*

The Fix

His early memories were probably no longer reliable: his
mother lying on the bed with her well-muscled legs wide apart, her
skirt up to her stomach, her cunt smiling.

"You'll have to be quick today. Your father's coming home early."

The school satchel, hastily dumped on the dressing table, contained his homework: the unified field theory that he had eventually destroyed, save for the single copy on a shelf somewhere in the Vatican Library.

Jerry took out his cigar case and selected an Upmann. Time moved swiftly and erratically these days. With the little silver syringe he cut the cigar and lit it, staring through the rain-dappled window at the soft summer landscaping surrounding his isolated Tudor Mansion. It had been some while since he had last visited the West Country.

He adjusted the stiff white shirt cuffs projecting an inch beyond the sleeves of his black car coat, placed his hand near his heart and shifted the shoulder holster slightly to make it lie more comfortably. Even the assassination business was getting complicated.

On the Job

"The conflicting time streams of the 20th century were mirrored in Jerry Cornelius." – Early reference

At the Time Centre

Alvarez, a man of substance, sniggered at Jerry as they climbed into their orange overalls. Jerry pursed his lips good-humouredly. The brightly coloured lab was humming with activity and all the screens gleamed. Alvarez winked.

"Will you want the use of the mirror tonight, Mr Cornelius?"

"No thanks, Alvarez. Enough's enough, right?"

"Whatever you say, though there's not much time left."

"Whichever – we'll get by."

They strolled towards the machine, a shimmering web of crimson and gold, so sophisticated.

With some poise Alvarez adjusted a dial, darting a glance at Jerry who seated himself, placed the tips of his fingers on his forehead, and stared into the shimmering web.

"How would you like it, Mr Cornelius?"

"Medium," Jerry said.

As Alvarez busied himself with the little controls he murmured incidentally. "Do you think mouth-to-mouth fertilisation will make much difference, sir? What's your bet? How do you fancy their chances?"

Jerry didn't bother to reply. The web was beginning to bulge near $N\frac{1}{4}E$.

"Look to your helm, Mr Alvarez."

"Aye, eye, sir."

The Dessert

Jerry hated needling a dead man, but it was necessary. He looked down at the twice-killed corpse of Borman, the first Nazi astronaut. The riding britches had been pulled below his thighs. Perhaps it had been a last minute attempt to gain sympathy, Jerry thought, when Borman had unbuttoned the britches to expose the thin white scars on his pelvis and genitals.

The seedy Sherman Oaks apartment was still in semi-darkness. Borman had been watching a cartoon show when Jerry had called. An arsenical Bugs Bunny leapt along a mildew-coloured cliff.

Jerry turned off the cheap TV and left.

Tense

Curling his hair with his fingers, Jerry looked quizzically at the mirror. Then he looked hard. But it didn't work.

The mirror.

He pinched the tip of his nose.

Reflecting on the enigma, he got into his purple brocade bellbottoms, his deep crimson shirt, and delicately strapped on his heater, setting the holster comfortably on his hip.

The room was cool, with white walls, a gold carpet, a low glass table in the middle of the floor.

From the floor, Catty Ley reached smoothly up to stroke his trousers. "You got . . .?"

She wore the bra that showed her nipples, the black stockings, the mauve garters and boots. "You object . . ."

"Oh, yes."

"Darling."

He smiled, began to comb his hair, taking the long strands down so that they framed his face. "There's been a bulge," he said, "and it's still bulging. We're trying to do something about it. Fuck it."

"A rapture?"

"Who's to say?"

"An eruption?"

"Perhaps."

"Will you be needing me for anything?"

"It depends how everything goes."

"Jerry!"

"Catty . . ."

It was time to get back to the **Time Centre.**

Facts

There were two sexes, he thought, *plus permutations. There is death, there is fear, there is time. There is birth, serenity, and time. There is identity, maybe. There is conflict. Robbed of their ambiguities, things cease to exist. Time, as always, was the filter.*

Double Lightning

A whole school of ships lay at anchor in the Bay and the tall cranes on the dockside formed a long wedding arch for Jerry as he walked lightly towards the pier where *Teddy Bear* was berthed. The sun shone on the rainbow oil, on the crisp, white shrouds of the ship, on the schooner's bright brass. She was a beautiful vessel, built in 1920 for Shang Chien, the playboy warlord, who had sailed her regularly from the opium-rich ports of the China seas to Monte Carlo until Mao had paid him off to settle in France where he had recently died.

What was the ship doing in Frisco?

Jerry went aboard.

A tatty jack tar greeted him, rolling along the deck whistling *So Sad.*

"Master in the cabin?" Jerry asked. Something was shaping.

The sailor sighed. "Won't be." He went to the rail and ran his fingers along the brasswork. He gave Jerry a secret, sardonic look. "Larger things have come up."

The sailor didn't stop him as he sauntered to the main companionway and descended.

The schooner's fittings were really Edwardian; all guilt and redplush. Jerry's feet sank into the soft carpet. He withdrew them, moving with difficulty. Finding the cabin he walked in, sniffing the musty air. Korean tapestries in the manner of Chong Son covered the walls; ceramics – mainly Yi dynasty – were fixed on all the shelves. He knew at once that, for the moment at least, the action was elsewhere. But where?

As he made his way back he saw that the holes his feet had made were filling with masses of white maggots. He grinned. There was no doubt in his mind: sooner or later the schooner would be scuppered by someone. A woman? He paused, trying to get the feel of it. Yes, possibly a woman. He lit an Upmann. The maggots began to squirm over his shoes. He moved on.

As he reached the gangplank, the sailor reappeared.

"You know what's wrong with you . . ." the sailor began.

"Save it, sailor."

Jerry swung down to the pier, making it fast to where his Phantom III was parked.

He got the big car going. His spirits had risen considerably.

"It's all essential," he laughed.

Facts

It was so elusive. There were events that frightened him; relationships that he could not cope with directly. Were his own actions creating some particular kind of alchemy?

There was birth.

Beckett had written a letter to a friend. "What can I do? Everything I touch turns to art in my hands."

After thirty or forty years, even Duchamp's ready-mades had come to be objects of interest for him.

Tolerance. Tension. Integrity. Why was he running away?

I am tired, he thought; exhausted. But he had to finish the job in hand.

There was murder.

The Map

Jerry studied the map. His father would have known what to do, and he would have done the right or the wrong thing.

The map was a little faded in places, but it offered a clue.

Now he had to wait for a phone call.

"The next great American hero will be a Communist"

Jerry grinned as he drove along. The recent discovery of sex and drugs had taken their minds off the essential problems. Time was silting up. Sooner or later there would be the Flood and then, with a spot of luck, everything would be cooler. It was his job to get the muck shifted as fast as possible. It was a dirty but essentially satisfying job.

His car hit an old man with an extraordinary resemblance to Walt Disney's Pinocchio. No, there was an even closer likeness. He got it. Richard Nixon. He roared with laughter.

It had all started to work out nice with the folding, at long last, of *The Saturday Evening Post*.

Development I

Really, one only had to wait for death to kiss the bastards. Those who wouldn't die had to be killed. Kinetically, of course, it was very simple.

He switched on the car radio and got *Your Mother Should Know* by the Beatles.

Fact

There was death.

Supposition

You had to keep your eye on the facts.

Falsehood

There was no such thing as falsehood.

Uncomfortable Visions

Toronto was grey, square and solid. The sun wasn't shining and the traffic wasn't moving. There was a crowd in the street.

Andrew Wells was due to speak at and inspire the big Civil Rights Convention in Toronto where all the American exiles (or "yellow bellies" as they were known) had gathered.

True to the spirit of convention, Andrew, dressed in a neat grey business suit, addressed the exiles and their friends from a balcony on the second floor of Rochdale College, the squarest block in the city. From the roof of the building opposite Jerry had an excellent view of the balcony, the crowd below, and the speaker. Jerry was dressed in the full ceremonial uniform of a Royal Canadian Mounted Policeman. The only difference was that the gun in the neat leather holster on his belt was his trusty heater.

As Andrew began his conventional address concerning universal brotherhood, freedom and the New Apocalypse, Jerry drew the heater, levelled it on his crooked left arm, sighted down it and burned Andrew right in the middle of his black mouth, moving the beam about to cauterize the face. Naturally, there wasn't much blood.

He got into the Kamov Ka-15 helicopter and ascended to the clouds where he made a quick getaway, wondering which poor bastard would claim the credit this time.

Muscle Trouble

In mutable times like these, thought Jerry as he walked back into Lionel Himmler's Blue Spot Bar, everything was possible and nothing was likely. His friend Albert the émigré nodded to him from the shadowy corner by the bar, lifting his glass of schnapps in the strobelight, saluting both Jerry and the stripper on the stage.

Jerry flickered to a table, sat down and ordered scotch and milk. Once history ceased to be seen in linear terms, it ceased to be made in linear terms. He glanced at his new watch. It consisted of eight yellow arrows radiating from a purple central hub. There were no figures marked on it, but the arrows went rapidly round and round. He could check the time only in relation to the speed at which the arrows moved. The arrows were moving very rapidly now.

Albert finished his schnapps, wiped his hands over his shaggy, grey beard and staggered towards the Wardour Street exit of the bar, on his way back to his sad little bedsitter decorated from floor to ceiling with dusty old charts, sheets of equations and eccentric geometric figures.

In these days of temporal and social breakdown the human psyche suffered enormously. Jerry felt sorry for the little Jew. History had destroyed him.

The drums stopped beating. The strobe gave way to conventional lighting. Suddenly it seemed he was the only customer. The waiter arrived, put his drink down, tucking the bill under the glass.

"How about that – Symphony Sal," said the MC, coming on clapping. "Give her a big hand," he said quietly, looking around the deserted bar. "Give her a big hand," he told Jerry.

Jerry started to clap.

The MC went away. The bar was silent.

Only in dreams did karma continue to have any meaning, thought Jerry. Or, at least, so it sometimes seemed.

He turned.

She was standing there in the doorway, smiling at him, her wide-brimmed hat like a halo. A Tory woman in garden party good taste.

She came to his table and picked up the tag with her gloved fingers.

"I'll take that, sonny."

The gloves were of blue lace, up to the elbow. She wore a dark blue cotton suit that matched her hat. Her hair was black and her oval face was beautiful. She parted her lips.

"So?" said Jerry.

"Soon," she purred. "I've got some answers for you. Are you interested?"

"What do you think?"

She glanced demurely at her blue shoes. "To stop now would severely complicate things. You and your friends had better call it a day. You could always come in with me."

"In there?" Jerry shook his head.

"It's not so different." She gave him a hard little smile.

"About as different as yin from yang. Sure." Jerry reached out and placed his right palm hard against her stomach. She shrugged.

"It's too late, I think," she said. "We should have got together earlier." With a movement of her hips she took a small step away from him.

"You could always get some new sex stars, couldn't you?" Jerry sipped his scotch and milk.

"Certainly."

"Are the current ones essential?"

She smiled more openly and gave him a candid look. "I see. You know a lot, Mr Cornelius."

"My job."

"And you want a new one?"

"Maybe."

"I'm Lady Susan Sunday," she said.

"Lady Sue."

She shrugged. "You're out of luck, I think. We're really moving. Frightfully nice to have met you, Mr Cornelius."

Jerry watched her pay the waiter. He knew her from the file. A close associate of his old enemy Captain Maxwell, from the Burma and China days. The opposition was organising a freeze, if he wasn't mistaken. She had told him everything. A stasis situation. He sniffed.

When she had gone, he went up to the bar. "Have you a mirror?"

"Lovely for you," said the barman.

The Pieces

When he got back, Catty was still in her uniform. He took her soft shoulders and kissed her on the mouth. He put his hands in her pants.

"Look," she said, waving at the centre of the room where an ornate crystal chess set was laid out on a low table. "Want a game?"

"I can't play chess," he said.

"Oh, fuck," she said.

He regarded her with compassionate anticipation. "You'd better fetch me those levitation reports," he said.

The Music of Time

The road was straight and white between avenues of cedars and poplars. Jerry idled along doing forty.

The Inkspots were singing *Beautiful Dreamer* on the Duesenberg's tapes. It amused Jerry to match his tapes to his cars. They finished that one and began *How Deep is the Ocean?*

On the seat beside him Jerry had a Grimshaw guitar with the shaped resonator. They had appeared just too late and had been quickly superseded by the electric guitar. Now George Formby's ukulele thrummed.

"In a young lady's bedroom I went by mistake
My intentions were honest you see
But she shouted with laughter,
I know what you're after:
It's me Auntie Maggie's remedy."

1957 had marked the end of the world Jerry had been born into. Adapting was difficult. He had to admit that he had had special advantages. Already people were beginning to talk about him as "The Messiah of the Age of Science" and a lot of apocryphal stories were circulating. He laughed. He wasn't the archetype. He was a stereotype.

Still, he did what he could.

Science, after all, was a much more sophisticated form of superstition than religion.

After this little episode was completed (if "completed" was the word) he would go and relax among that particularly degenerate tribe of headhunters who had adopted him on his last visit to New Guinea.

He smiled as large drops of rain hit the windscreen and were vaporised. On that trip he had been responsible for starting at least eight new cargo cults.

Don't Let Me Down

That great big woman had almost been the death of him. There had been so much of her. A hungry woman who had fed his own greed. He sucked breath through clenched teeth at the memory, expelled a shivering sigh.

He had probably been the last of the really innocent mother-fuckers. It had been her slaughter, not society, that had put a stop to it. His funny old father, Dr Cornelius (a loyable eccentric, a visionary in his own way), had killed her when she got cancer of the cervix, running a white-hot poker into her cunt without so much as a by-your-leave.

His eyes softened nostalgically. He remembered her wit.

Once, when his sister Catherine had come out with a particularly sour remark, his mother had rounded on her from the table where she had been cutting up onions.

"Say that again, love, and I'll carve me fucking name on your womb."

As it turned out, she'd made something of a prophetic retort.

His childhood had been, until his voluntary entry into the Jesuit seminary, an unspoiled and relatively uncomplicated one. But he couldn't complain. It had been much more interesting than many.

He turned the Duesenberg into a side lane. Through the twilight he could see the silhouette of the Tudor Mansion. He needed a fresh car coat. The brown leather one, in the circumstances.

Get Back

An expectancy of change grew out of the dynamic of a search for the "new politics", a kind of quest-epic which had to end on schedule on 5 November. Disappointment followed when the search produced nothing new. All the found objects were cast in old forms. Humphrey's coalition was virtually indistinguishable from Roosevelts's, Truman's or Johnson's – except that crucial sections had fallen away. McCarthy and Nixon were both relying on a Fifties phenomenon – the ascendancy of the surburban elite. John Kennedy had used that class already in 1960. In their separate ways, Nixon and McCarthy both sought its allegiance, and, if they had contested each other directly, 1968 would have been a delayed-replay of 1960. McCarthy would probably have won: precisely because he could recapture the old spirit, not because he could fashion the new. – Andrew Kopkind, *America: the Mixed Curse*

Pour les originaux

Jerry looked through the mail that had accumulated since he had been away.

Outside the French windows the sky was overcast and rain still swished among the oaks. Softly from the stereo came the Beatles' *Only a Northern Song*.

There was a request to open a local fête. It was from the vicar of the village church and began "I know you have a very full schedule but . . ." He was a month behind on his Telstar rental and there was a final demand from the firm who had supplied the aircraft carrier which he had lost on the abortive Antarctic expedition where they had failed to find the opening to Pellucidar. A pot scheme if ever there had been one.

A folded sheet marked *Plattegrond van Amsterdam*. Several postcards without messages.

At last he found what he'd been expecting. The envelope had been resealed and forwarded from his Ladbroke Grove convent. He opened it and shook out the contents.

A torn envelope. Small brown manilla with the address ripped off and a stamp that said "Join the sun set in Eastbourne this year". A fivepenny stamp, postmarked Eastbourne, Sussex, the date indecipherable. On the back, three words: Assassin – Assassin – Assassin.

An Imperial Reply Coupon stamped Juliasdale, Rhodesia,

23rd Jan. '69: "Valid only for exchange within the British Empire. Southern Rhodesia. Selling 3d price. This coupon may be exchanged in any part of the BRITISH EMPIRE for a postage stamp or stamps representing the postage on a single rate letter to a destination within the Empire. Exceptionally the exchange value in India and Burma is 2½ annas." The engraving, blue on oatmeal, was of a standing Britannia looking out over the sea at a square-rigged sailing ship.

An empty book match folder marked UCS.

A postcard with a fourpenny Concorde stamp postmarked Weston-S-Mare, Somerset, 15 Apr. 1969. It showed a big wave breaking on a rock and the caption read: "The Cornish Seas. A study of the waves breaking on the rocks. There is nothing but the open Atlantic between the Cornish coast and America: A Natural Colour Photograph."

The last item was a rather dog-eared sheet of paper, folded several times and secured with a paper clip. Jerry removed the paper clip and unfolded the paper.

There was a message. A single handwritten line in separated upper and lower case letters. "The ship is yours. B."

Jerry frowned and put the various bits and pieces back into the envelope. He sipped his mug of black coffee as the Beatles sang *Altogether Now* and he studied the envelope to see if it gave him any further clues. It had four stamps on it. A fivepenny showing the *Queen Elizabeth II*; a shilling showing the RMS *Mauretania*; another shilling showing the SS *Great Britain*. It bore his Ladbroke Grove address and the forwarding number circled in blue ballpoint – 93. In the top left-hand corner was written in black felt pen: Urgent Special Delivery. The fourth stamp was in the bottom right-hand corner. Another fourpenny Concorde.

What was he to make of it?

There was nothing else but to go down to the harbour in the morning and look at the ships.

For the rest of the evening, before he went to bed, he read the comic strip serial in his back issues of *International Times*. The strip was called *The Adventures of Jerry Cornelius. The English Assassin.*

Maybe it would add up to something, after all.

The Golden Apples of the Sun

Dylan and the rest, unable to face the implications of their own subject matter, had beaten a quick retreat. Those few whom they had urged on were left stranded, staring around them in bewilderment.

Now the times, had, indeed, changed. But the prophets had not. They had only been able to predict – not adapt.

Multi-value logic.

Was it logic, in any real sense, at all?

Or was he really only imposing his own vision on reality; a vision so strong that, for a short time, it would seem to be confirmed by the events around him.

Be that as it may, it was time for some action. He stripped and cleaned his needle-gun, drew on his black car coat, his black bell-bottoms, his white shirt with the Bastille-style collar, put the gun in its case, put the case in his pocket, left the Tudor Mansion, locked the doors behind him, looked up at the morning sun slanting through the clouds, and walked on his cuban-heeled feet towards the blue and sparkling sea.

In his dress and his methods of operation he, too, was an anachronism. But he knew no other way. Perhaps there would, in human terms, never be another way. Equilibrium had to be maintained somehow and as far as Jerry was concerned, only the ontologists had any kind of satisfactory answer.

The New Man

Pope Paul turned saint-slayer in the interests of historical accuracy. Out go the saints whose existence is now doubted. St Barbara, whose name has been given to millions of girls and an American city, is struck off. So are Susanna, Boniface of Tarsus, Ursula and her fellow martyrs. An English saint whose existence cannot be doubted moves into the Calendar . . .
– *Sun,* 10 May 1969

Capacity

At Harbour Street Jerry paused to rest. His boots weren't suitable for cobbled lanes.

There was hardly anyone about in the little Cornish village. A smell of fish, a few inshore trawlermen mending their nets, white stone walls of the cottages, grey slate roofs, the masts of the boats that had not yet put out to sea.

Looking down the narrow street at the harbour and beyond it, Jerry saw the yacht anchored at the far end of the stone mole that had been built during the village's better days.

It was *Teddy Bear*. The yacht had been given a lick of fresh white paint. A corpse of a boat. Is that where the meeting was to take place?

He began to trudge along the mole. The mole was also cobbled. His feet were killing him.

Development II

The War is Over

The kind of chromosomes a person has is called his genotype, and the appearance of a person is called his phenotype. Thus, males have the genotype XY and the phenotype male. Women have the genotype XX and the phenotype female. . . . In every war in history there must have been a considerable flow of genes one way or another. Whether the genes of the victors or of the vanquished have increased most is a debatable point.
– Papazian, *Modern Genetics*

Miss Brunner

The boat smelled as if she had been fouled by a score of cats. Jerry stood on the rotting deck and waited.

Eventually Miss Brunner emerged from the wheelhouse. She was dressed as severely as ever in a Cardin trouser suit as dated as Jerry's own clothes. She held a baby in her crooked right arm, a Smith & Wesson .44 revolver in her left hand.

She gave him a bent smile. "Good morning, Mr Cornelius. So our paths come together again."

"I got your note. What's up, Miss Brunner?"

She shook her short red hair in the wind and turned her feline face down to regard the baby.

"Do you like children, Mr Cornelius?"

"It depends." Jerry moved to look at the baby and was shocked.

"It's got your eyes and mouth, hasn't it?" said Miss Brunner. She offered it to him. "Would you like to hold it?"

He took a wary step backward. She shrugged and tossed the little creature far out over the rail. He heard it hit the water, whine, gurgle.

"I only hung on to it in case you'd want to have it," she said apologetically. "Okay, Mr Cornelius. Let's get down to business."

"I might have kept it," Jerry said feelingly. "You didn't give me much of a chance to consider."

"Oh, really, Mr Cornelius. You should be able to make up your mind more quickly than that. Are you going soft?"

"Just crumbling a little, at the moment."

"Ah well, it's all written in the quasars, I suppose. Come along."

He followed her down the companionway, along the passage and into the cabin decorated with the Korean tapestries.

"Could we have a porthole open?" Jerry asked.

Pettishly Miss Brunner flung open a porthole. "I didn't know you cared that much for fresh air."

"It's to do with my upbringing." Jerry saw that there were charts unfolded on the ornate mother-of-pearl chart table. He gave them the once-over. A cockroach crawled across a big detailed plan of Hyde Park.

"I suppose you know it's Maxwell and his gang," Miss Brunner said. "Trying the old diversion game again. I don't know who that woman thinks she is . . ." She glared at Jerry and turned her head to stare out of the porthole. "They're building up a sex scene that could set us back by I don't know how long. Essentially a red herring – but we'll have to nip it in the bud, if we can. Fight fire with fire. I'm not unsympathetic, Mr Cornelius . . ."

"Any clues?" Jerry lit an Upmann in the hope that it would overlay some of the stink.

Miss Brunner made an agitated gesture.

He gave her a cool, slightly contemptuous look. She couldn't work that one on him. There was no background.

She crossed rapidly to a locker set high in the bulkhead near the door. Taking something from the locker she tossed it to him. "Recognise that?"

Jerry turned the dildo in his hands. It had a crude, unaesthetic feel to it. "Don't know. It looks slightly familiar, but . . ."

"Have a look at the stem."

Jerry stared closely at the stem. A brand name. *Maxwell's Deviant Devices, London, W.8.*

"Overloaded. He's not happy in his work. That links it with the captain, all right," Jerry agreed.

She brought something else out of the locker and put it on the chart table. It was a vial of processed DNA.

"Makes sense," said Jerry. "They're attempting to slow down the transmogrification by fucking about with identity – concentrating on the heaviest sex angles they can find. It's the easiest way, of course. But crude. I can't believe that anyone these days . . . Such an old trick . . ."

"But it could be an effective one. You know how unstable things have been getting since 1965. These people are pre-1950!"

They laughed together.

"I'm serious, though," added Miss Brunner, sitting down. "They won't even use chrono-barometers."

"Bugger me. How do they tell the Time?"

"They don't admit it's here. It's our main advantage, of course."

Fact

There were a great many instincts in common between *homo sapiens* and the other animals.

As Barrington Bayley had pointed out in his book *Structural Dynamism*, man was not an intelligent animal. He was an animal with intelligence that he could apply to some, not all, of his activities.

Supposition

$E = mc^2$

Falsehood

Truth is absolute.

Cutting the Mustard

Miss Brunner handed him a beef sandwich. He bit it and grimaced. "It tastes of grass."

"It's all a question of how you process it, I suppose," she said.

She began to strap on her underclothes. "Well, that's our pact sealed. Where do you intend to go from here?"

"Back to London first. Then I'll start sniffing around."

She darted him an admiring look.

"You're coarse, darling – but you know how to get down to the nitty gritty."

"I don't suppose you'll be around when the shit hits the fan."

"You never know. But we'd better say goodbye, just in case."

She handed him a cardboard carton full of old Beatles singles and a photograph. "Don't lose it. It's our only contact."

"You anticipate a wax situation?"

"Maybe something a little more sophisticated than that. Is your equipment okay?"

"Ready to go."

"Oh, sweetie . . ."

She fell on his erection.

Electric Ladyland

Jerry took the Kamov Ka-15 to London. From there he would call Oxford.

The sound of the 'copter's rotors drummed in his ears. The fields fled by below. He didn't care for this sort of backtracking operation.

He would need Catty. And he would need one of them. A particular one.

He'd better check his circuits and get in any chemicals he was short on. He sighed, knowing that he would soon be immersed, but not relishing the prospect.

Reaching to the far side of the cockpit, he adjusted the Ellison meter.

Ladbroke Grove lay ahead. He began to drop her down.

If his mother hadn't taken it into her head that he should have a hobby, he wouldn't be in this situation now. He supposed he was grateful, really.

Consequences

When he had made the phone call, Jerry looked through his mother's recipe books to refresh his memory.

Then he made a list of ingredients.

Captain Maxwell

Captain Maxwell left the Austin Princess and crossed the grass verge at the agreed point. They were meeting on the banks of the Cam, just to the north east of Cambridge. The tow-path was lined with fishermen. The river was full of punts. It was a lovely day.

"I thought this would constitute neutral territory, old boy." Maxwell smiled as he came briskly up to where Jerry was standing watching an angler.

"Neutral territory?" Jerry looked up absently.

Maxwell had lost weight since Jerry had last seen him. He wore a Harris Tweed jacket with leather patches on the sleeves and leather bands round the cuffs, cream cricket flannels, an old Etonian tie. His lips were as red as ever, his round face as bland. "How are you, old chap? I thought you were dead!" He insinuated a smile on to his features. "What can I do for you? Say the word."

"I felt like a chat," said Jerry. Although the day was warm, he wore his double-breasted black car coat buttoned up and his hands were in his pockets. "You seem to have done well for yourself since Burma."

"I can't complain, old sport."

"You've expanded your business interests, I hear. Getting the export market."

"You could put it like that. The American tie-up with Hunt seems to be working all right."

Maxwell put his hand on Jerry's elbow and they began to trudge along the tow-path, side by side. The air was full of sweet summer smells. Crickets chirped and bees buzzed.

"I was talking to the bishop about you only the other day," continued Maxwell. "He doesn't approve of you at all, old son." He gave a short, plummy laugh. "I told him it was nothing more than high spirits. 'Spawn of the Antichrist', indeed!"

Jerry grinned.

Maxwell glanced at him, looked disconcerted, cleared his throat. "You know the bishop. A bit of a romantic. A bit High Church, too, for my taste. Since I became PM, I've had to think about things like that."

"How is the government?"

"Oh, well – it's *small*, y'know, but generally pretty effective in what it tries to do, I think."

"I haven't seen much about it recently."

"We don't often get into the media these days, of course. But we remain realistic. In the meantime we're thinking of building a smaller House of Commons. The one we're using now can accommodate over a hundred members. It's far too big for us to manage." Maxwell stopped by the river and kicked at a stone. "But we'll see, we'll see . . ."

"You're hoping people will get interested in politics again?"

"I *am* rather hoping that, old boy, yes." Maxwell tried to cover up a sudden secretive expression.

"But for politics, they need surrogates . . ."

Maxwell looked up sharply. "If you mean *issues* – I think we can find *issues* for them all right."

Jerry nodded. "On the other hand, captain, you can't turn back the clock, can you?"

"Don't intend to, old boy. I'm thinking of the future. The swing of the pendulum, you know."

Jerry began to giggle uncontrollably.

He stepped into a passing punt. "Well, so long, captain."

"TTFN, old chap. Hope I could assist . . ."

Jerry developed hiccups. He fell backwards into the water.

"Oh, shit!" he laughed. He signalled for his helicopter to come down and pick him up.

The only depressing thing about the encounter was that briefly, at any rate, he had to take the captain's plans seriously.

Popcorn

Jerry tuned his guitar to modal G and played *Old Macdonald Had a Farm* with a Far Eastern feeling.

He looked through the leaded and barred window of the converted convent that was his Ladbroke Grove HQ. Maxwell's opium business was booming. The captain disguised his consignments as penicillin and anti-tetanus serum and shipped them mainly to underdeveloped nations. They were, in fact, developing rapidly with the captain's help.

The sun went in. It began to rain.

Jerry got up and put on his coat. Then he went down the long, dark staircase to the front door and out into the courtyard where he climbed into his Phantom VI.

As he drove down Ladbroke Grove, he pulled out the dusty drawer in the dashboard containing the .45 player and stacked the old Beatles singles on to it. *The Inner Light* began to play. Jerry smiled, taking a hand-rolled from the nearby tray and sticking the liquorice paper between his lips. It was all such a long time ago. But he had to go through with it.

He remembered the Burma days.

Every gun makes its own tune . . .

It wasn't the first time Maxwell had succeeded in buggering the equilibrium. But in those days he hadn't liked working with women.

Jerry cheered up at the prospect of his next action.

Cause and Effect

The three men who took the Apollo 8 spaceship on its Christmas journey round the moon were awarded a trophy in London yesterday – for providing "the most memorable colour TV moment of the past year or any other year". . . . Others who were honoured for the year's best achievements in colour TV were comedian Marty Feldman and actress Suzanne Neeve. Derek Nimmo, famous for his parts in "Oh Brother" and "All Gas and Gaiters" won the Royal Television Society's silver medal for "outstanding artistic achievement in front of the camera". – *Sun*, 10 May 1969

Sweet Child

Jerry got what he needed. It was the last thing on his list.

In Holland Park he wandered hand in hand with Helen who was happy. Her long blonde hair was thick and delicate and her little mini-dress had a gold chain around the waist. Her breasts were sixteen years old and full and she was just plump enough all over. She had a great big red mouth and delicious teeth and huge dark eyes that were full of surprises.

It was a silent summer day and all the trees were green and still and Jerry sang and sprang along the leafy paths.

Helen, behind him, gave a slightly condescending smile.

Jerry shrugged and folded his arms across his chest, turning. He narrowed his eyes and said softly, "Do you love me, Helen?"

"More or less."

"More or less?"

"Oh, Jerry!" She laughed.

He looked about him, through the trees. The park was deserted.

He drew his needle-gun.

Helen looked at it curiously. "You are silly, Jerry."

He gestured with his weapon.

"Come here, Helen."

She stepped lightly towards him. With his left hand he reached out and felt below her pelvis. He shook his head.

"Is that yours?"

"Of course it's mine."

"I mean real or false?"

"Who can say?"

"Take it off."

She pulled up her skirt and undid the little pin that released it into her hand. She gave it to him. "I feel funny now," she said. "More or less."

"You'd better go ahead of me," said Jerry, replacing his needle-gun.

Resolution

Because man is an animal, movement is most important for him . . . Long distance running is particularly good training in perseverance. – Mao Tse-Tung, *Hsin ch'ing-nien*, April 1917

Customs

His mouth was full of blood. He popped the last of the liver down his throat and sucked his lower lip, appraising Helen, who stood shivering in the centre of the pentagram. Then he took the speakers and placed one on each of the star's five points, turned to the console on the wall and switched on.

Sparks leapt from point to point and settled into a blue-green flow. Helen hugged her naked breasts.

"Keep your arms at your sides, please," said Miss Brunner from the darkness on the other side of the lab.

"It's only a temporal circuit. There's nothing to worry about yet."

Jerry turned a dial. Softly, at first, the music issued from the speakers. Jimi Hendrix's *Still Raining, Still Dreaming*. Helen began to sway to the sound.

Jerry switched tracks, studying the girl carefully. He got The Deep Fix and *Laughing Gods*. She jerked, her eyes glazing.

Jerry gave Miss Brunner the thumbs up sign, turned off the power for a moment to let her into the pentagram, switched on and increased the volume.

His eyes stopped blinking. His face was bathed in the blue-green glow as he watched Miss Brunner move in on the girl.

Grand Guignol

It was telekinesis of a sort, Jerry supposed. You had to act it all out. That was the drag, sometimes. Still – desperate days, desperate measures.

When the drums started to beat, you had to dance.

Na Chia

Delicately Jerry removed Catty's lights and threw them steaming into the kidney dish. Miss Brunner picked up the dish and left the room. "I'll be getting on with these."

"Okay," said Jerry. His job involved much more precise surgery, for he was attempting nothing less than necromancy.

And there wasn't much time.

T'si i

He pumped Catty's corpse full of methane wishing that Miss Brunner had not used up Helen so completely. This was the dark period. The low point. Even if they were successful in cleaning up the Maxwell problem, there was still much to do.

A kalpa, after all, was a kalpa. It sometimes seemed it would last forever. Nonetheless, he would be glad when this particular job was wound up.

The drums were beating faster now. His pulse-rate rose, his temperature increased. In the strobe light his face was flushed, his eyes burning, and there was a rim of blood around his lips. The lab was in chaos where he had ransacked it in his haste, searching out the equipment and chemicals he needed.

Squatting by the gas cylinder, he howled along with The Deep Fix.

Scream

"Belphegor!" shrieked Maxwell as Jerry appeared in the window, his car coat unbuttoned and flapping in the sudden wind, his heater in his hand.

Jerry was incapable of speech now. His glowing eyes scanned

the opulent room and he remained stock-still, framed against the full moon.

He would never know if Maxwell had identified him as Belphegor or whether that was who the captain had called for. He crouched.

He sprang.

The prime minister ran across the room. From somewhere the Beatles began to sing *Sexy Sadie*. Maxwell touched the door handle and whimpered.

Jerry burned him.

Then, while Maxwell was still hot, he bit off everything he could find.

This was politics with a vengeance.

Baby's in Black

Jerry flattened the accelerator. The world swam with blood. Walpurgis Eve. Trees and houses flashed past.

The breath hissed in through his tight fangs.

Gradually the drums slowed their tempo and Jerry cooled, dropped down to sixty and began to pick his teeth.

A nervous tick. He couldn't help laughing.

Anarchists in Love

He stopped off at the tenement in Robert Street on the borders of Soho. The house was empty now. It had been condemned for years. He pushed open the broken door and entered the damp darkness, treading the worm-eaten boards. His mother had claimed that this was where he had been born, with thick hair down to his shoulders and a full set of teeth, dragged feet first into the world. But towards the end his memory had been better than hers, though by no means reliable.

He struck a match, frowning, trod the groaning stairs to the first floor and found two tall black candles in bronze holders screwed on either side of the entrance to the room he had come to see. He lit the candles.

The place was being used. Neat symbols had been carved in

the walls and there were signs of recent occupation. Rats had been crucified near the candles. Some of them were still alive, moving feebly. An early portrait of himself, framed between two sheets of dark glass, hung on the door.

So the place had already become a shrine of some kind.

Below the portrait was a row of equations, quoted from one of his books. Jerry felt sick. Standing by the room he might have been born in, he bent and vomited out the blood that had bloated his stomach.

Weakly, he stumbled down the stairs and into the festering street.

They had taken the hub caps off his car. He glanced around, conscious of eyes peering at him. He buttoned his coat about his body, got into the driving seat and started the engine.

Perhaps the future would forget him. It had better for its own sake. He was, after all, only standing in until something better turned up.

Mrs Cornelius

After his mother's death they had moved, finally, to his father's fake Le Corbusier château. Somehow Jerry had always identified the house with his misfortune, though there was no particular evidence to support the idea.

The brain and the womb. Which had created him?

Perhaps neither.

She had begun to claim, as the cancer became more painful, that he had not been conceived by his father. His father had denied this.

"Who else would want to fuck you?" he used to say.

This of course had amused Jerry.

There had been a lot of laughter in the family in those days. Catherine, his brother Frank, his mother and father. Each had a particular kind of humour which had complemented that of the others.

But enough of the past.

He saw Miss Brunner bathed in his headlights and stopped the car.

"Perhaps you could drop me off at the coast," she said as she climbed in beside him. "The rest is up to you."

He smiled sweetly.

"Maxwell's out of it for the time being, I take it," said Miss Brunner. "There's only the residual bits and pieces to tidy up. Then the job's over."

"I suppose so."

The drums had started up again.

His and Hers

Then is there no such thing as justice? . . . His scientific mind is irradiated by this idea. Yet surely the question is, in itself, scientific, psychological, moral, and can therefore be accepted without bias, however disturbing? Lost in these deliberations Dr Cornelius discovers he has arrived back at his own door.
– Thomas Mann, *Disorder and Early Sorrow*

The Sex Complex

Holland House was a sixteenth-century manor reconstructed as a façade in 1966. On the white battlements stood guards in yellow leather.

"Helen?" called one.

"Okay, Herschel."

They went through the iron doors and the floor began to sink under their feet, taking them down and down through crawling light.

At the bottom Jerry drew his heater and pushed what was left of the fake Helen through the opening into the huge hall where the freaks turned to glance at them before looking back at Lady Sue Sunday, still in her Tory set, who stood in an ornate pulpit at the far end.

"Helen!" Lady Sue looked prim.

"It was inconclusive," said what was left of the fake Helen defensively. "Really."

"S . . ."

Jerry glimmed Lady Sue's freaks. "Jesus," he said. There were little boys dressed as little girls. There were men dressed as women and women decked out like men in almost every detail. There were androgynes and hermaphrodites. There were little girls dressed as little boys. There were hugely muscled women and tiny, soft men.

"Irony, Lady Sue, is no substitute for imagination."

He shook his head and unbuttoned his car coat with his free hand.

Lady Sue put a glove to her lips.

"You're a naughty boy, Jerry. Naughty, naughty, naughty boy . . ."

Jerry laughed. "Evidently you never knew my mother."

Lady Sue scowled.

"Maxwell's had it," Jerry said. "I only dropped in to let you know. You can go home. It's all over."

"Naughty . . ."

"Oh, shut up." He raised his gun.

She licked her lips.

Jerry watched the urine as it began to drip from the floor of the pulpit. Lady Sue looked uncomfortable. She spread her arms to indicate her creatures.

Jerry sighed. "If you hadn't been so damned literal-minded . . ."

"You can accuse . . ." With an impatient gesture she touched a button on the pulpit's console. Little Richard music began to roar about the hall.

Jerry relaxed. No good getting excited.

"This is a one-way ticket," he called, waving his heater at the scene. "A line. Just a line."

"Who needs angles, you little horror?" She picked up her wide-brimmed blue hat and adjusted it on her head.

"At best a spiral," Jerry murmured wearily.

"A chain!" she cried. "A chain! Vitality! Don't you get it?"

"Off you go, Lady Sue."

Little Richard changed to James Brown. It was too much for Jerry. He began to race through the freaks towards the pulpit. The freaks kept touching him.

Lady Sue picked up a small vanity bag. "Well . . ." She was defeated. "Back to Hampstead, I suppose. Or . . ."

"You get a passage on a boat," he said. "The *Teddy Bear*. She's in the Pool of London now. Hurry up . . ."

"Why . . .?"

"Off you go. I might see you later."

She stepped out of the pulpit and walked towards the elevator immediately behind her – a golden cage. She got into the cage. It began to rise. Through the glass bottom Jerry could see right up her skirt, saw the damp pants.

When she had disappeared, he took his heater and burned down the pulpit. The lights began to fade, one by one.

The flaming pulpit gave him enough light to work. He cleaned up Lady Sue's mess, much more in sorrow than in anger. The mess recoiled then rushed at him. It was shouting. He backed away. Normally he would have used his heater, but he was now too full of melancholy. He had been very busy, after all.

They were never grateful.

The freaks pursued him to the lift; he got there first and went up fast.

He left Holland House and the guards shot at him as he raced through the door and out into the park. He ducked behind a statue and burned his initials into the chest of each of them.

That did it.

It was one for mother.

A Cure for Cancer

Jerry watched the *Teddy Bear* sail out into the calm oil of the Pool and start to sink.

Lady Sue leaned moodily on the rail, staring at him as the ship went down. Soon only her hat and the topmast were visible.

Jerry looked at his watch. It had almost stopped.

As he made his way back through the decrepit warehouses on the quayside he became aware of groups of figures standing in the shadows staring at him. Each of the figures was dressed in a moth-eaten black car coat he recognised as one of his cast-offs.

He shuddered and climbed into the Phantom VI.

His tongue was sweating. His heart was cold.

It had been a much tougher job that he expected.

Time off Time

"Adjustment okay," said Alvarez, coughing cheerfully. "Well, well, well . . ."

Jerry sat tired in his chair and inspected the shimmering web of crimson and gold. Apart from tiny and perfectly logical fluctuations in the outer strands, it was sweet and perfect.

"Aquilinus on tomorrow, isn't he?" Alvarez said as he tidied up.

Jerry nodded. He took a deep breath. "I'll have that mirror now. I'm looking forward to the change."

"That's a fact," said Alvarez.

The Sunset Perspective

A Moral Tale

1

Energy Quotient

Jerry Cornelius lay on his back in the sweet warm grass and looked across the sunny fields, down the hill towards the bright, smart sea. Overhead a flight of friendly Westland Whirlwinds chattered past, full of news. Soon it was silent again.

Jerry stretched and smiled.

A small fox terrier wriggled through the stile at the bottom of the hill and paused, wagging its tail at him.

A cloud moved in front of the sun and the day chilled. Jerry first watched the cloud and then watched the dog. He listened to the grasshoppers. They were scraping their legs together in the long grass by the hedge. He sniffed the wind.

It was all a matter of how you looked at it, thought Jerry, getting tired of waiting for the cloud to pass. He took a deep breath and sprang to his feet, dusting off his brown velvet bell-bottoms. The dog started to bark at him. On the other side of the hedge a cow's heavy body shook the leaves. In the distance a woman's voice called the dog. Things were moving in on him.

Time to be off.

Jerry buttoned up his black car coat and adjusted the collar to frame his pale face. He tramped along the footpath towards the village.

Seagulls screamed on the cliffs.

The church bell began to clank.

Jerry sighed. He reached the field where his Gates Twinjet was parked. He climbed in, revved the chopper's engine, and buzzed up into the relative peace of the skies over Cornwall, heading for London.

One was allowed such short periods of rest.

2

There was something in that blind, scarred face that was terrifying . . . He did not seem quite human. – W. Somerset Maugham, Preface, *Ashenden*

Time Quotient

When Jerry got to the Time Centre only Alvarez was on duty. He was boredly watching the chronographs, his bearded face a pale green in the light from the machines. He heard the footsteps and turned large, liquid brown eyes to regard Jerry.

"Looks salty," Jerry quipped, indicating the web model in the centre of the operations room. The web bulged badly along one of its straights.

"Miss Brunner said she'd see to the adjustments," Alvarez told him pettishly. Morale seemed to have declined since Jerry had been away. "But between you and me, Mr C, I think the whole bloody structure's going out of phase."

"Oh, come now . . ." Jerry made a few minor adjustments to Number Six 'graph, studied the results for a moment and then shrugged. "You haven't located the central cause of the bulge?"

"Miss Brunner's gone a bit funny, if you ask me."

Alvarez began to pick his teeth. "*On* the quiet," he added, "I'm pissed off with that bird."

"We all have our ups and downs, Mr Alvarez."

He went into the computing room. Miss Brunner's handbag was on her desk. There were some sheets of calculations near it, but they hadn't gone very far. The face of each wall was a section of the huge computer she had built. But the machine was dormant.

Miss Brunner had turned off the power.

That meant something. She was probably having another identity crisis.

But what had caused it?

3

Life proceeds amid an incessant network of signals . . . – George Steiner

Rise of the Total Energy Concept

Jerry finally managed to track Miss Brunner down. She was burying a goat in the Hyde Park crater and didn't see him come up and stand looking over the rim at her.

He watched as she mumbled to herself, hitching her Biba maxi-skirt up to her thighs and urinating on the new mound of earth.

"Well, you're really in a bad way, aren't you, Miss B?"

She raised her head. The red hair fell over her foxy face; the eyes were glassy. She hissed and smoothed down her muddy clothes. "It's a difficult situation, Mr Cornelius. We've got to try everything."

"Isn't this a bit dodgy?"

She picked up a stick and began to draw her usual mandala in the steaming earth. "If I can't be allowed to do my own job in my own way . . ."

"You've been working too hard."

"I've got eight toads and four newts buried around here!" She glared at him. "If you think I'm going to go round digging them up for you or anybody else . . ."

"Not necessary. Anyway, Alvarez obviously thinks we'll have to rephase."

"Bugger off."

"Look at yourself. You always revert to type in a crisis."

She paused, pushing back her hair and offering him a pitying smile. "Electricity's all you ever think about, isn't it? There are other methods, you know, which . . ."

Jerry dug inside his black car coat and took the needler from the shoulder holster. He waved it at her. "Come up out of there. You'll ruin your clothes."

She sniffed and began to climb, the loose earth falling away behind her.

He nudged her in the ribs with the needler and marched her to the Lear Steamer. Alvarez was in the driving seat. He had already got up enough pressure to start moving. Jerry sat beside Miss Brunner in the back seats of the car as it drove towards Bayswater Road.

"You reckoned the emanations vectored back to New York, didn't you?" he asked her. She had calmed down a bit now. "I read your initial calculations."

"New York was just involved in the first phase. I could have told you much more if you'd've let me finish with the goat . . ."

"I don't think goats are very efficient, Miss B."

"Well, what can we do about New York, anyway? We can't sort one AA Factor out from that lot there!"

"But the factor might sort us out."

4

WASHINGTON, Oct. 15 – Congress voted today to coin a new dollar that would honour former President, Dwight D. Eisenhower, but the Senate and the House of Representatives differed on whether it should be a silver dollar. Flourishing a letter from Mrs Eisenhower, a group of Western legislators got the Senate to override the Administration's proposal to produce a copper and nickel coin. A similar effort, backed by the same letter, failed in the House, which opted for the Administration's non-silver dollar. Mrs Eisenhower's letter disclosed that the former President had loved to collect and distribute silver dollars as mementos. – *New York Times*, 16 October 1969

Horror Rape of the Kidnapped Teenage Beauty

Jerry pared the black mixture of oil and blood from the nail of the little finger of his right hand and carefully licked his upper lip. Then he put both hands back on the steering wheel of the wavering Cadillac limousine. The car was as hard to control as a hovercraft. The sooner it was used up the better. He saw the toll barrier ahead on the multilane highway and brought the car down to seventy.

Cars pulled into the sides of the road as his siren sounded. Jerry's six outriders, in red and orange leather, moved into position at front and back of the Cadillac, their arms stretched on the crucifixes of their apehanger bars.

Jerry pressed a switch.

The Who began to sing *Christmas*. The sign hanging over the highway said DRIVERS WITH CORRECT CHANGE – THIS LANE.

Jerry paid his twenty-five cents at the turnpike and drove into New Jersey.

This was a noisy situation. There were either too many facts, or no facts at all – he couldn't be sure at this stage. But he had the feel of it. There was no doubt about one thing – it was a morality syndrome of the worst sort.

He checked his watch. The arrows whirled rapidly round the dial. Not much longer now.

The car lolloped along between the overgrown subsidy fields and the ramshackle internment centres.

Jerry lit a brown Sherman's Queen-Size Cigarettello.

Why Homosexuals Seek Jobs in Mental Hospitals

On George Washington Bridge Jerry decided to change the Cadillac for one of his outriders' BMW 750s. He stopped. The riders got off their bikes and parked them neatly in a line along the rail. Drivers behind them on the highway hooted, their horns dying as they approached, pulled up, looked elsewhere.

He slid from the car, was passed the leather helmet and mirror goggles by the blond who took his place in the driving seat.

Jerry tucked his black flare pants into the tops of his ornate Cherokee boots, buckled up and mounted the vacated bike. He kicked the starter and had reached eighty by the time he hit Manhattan and entered the island's thick haze of incense.

The Holy City

The babble of the charm-sellers, the fortune-tellers, the fakirs, the diviners, the oracles, the astrologers, the astromancers and necromancers mingled with the squeal of the tyres, the wail of the sirens, the caterwauling of the horns.

Corpses swayed on steel gibbets spanning the streets. Broadsheets pasted on the sides of buildings advertised spectacular entertainments, while on the roofs little parties of marauders crept among the chimneys and the collapsing neon signs.

The popping of distant gunfire occasionally signified a clash.

Shacked up for Slaughter!

Jerry and his riders got all the way down 7th Avenue to West 9th Street before they were blocked by a twelve-foot-high pile-up and had to abandon their bikes.

From what Jerry could see, the pile-up went down as far as Sheridan Square and West 4th St. The faggots had probably closed off the area again and were defending their territory. They had had a lot of bad luck up to now. Maybe this time they would be successful.

Jerry took out his glasses and scanned the fire escapes – sure enough, the faggots, sporting the stolen uniforms of the Tactical Riot Police, were lobbing B-H5 gas grenades into the tangled heaps of automobiles.

Sheltering under a sign saying DOLLARS BOUGHT AT COM-PETITIVE PRICES, Jerry watched for a few seconds.

It looked like a mince-over for the faggots.

My God, Wild Dogs are Attacking the Kids!

Eventually Jerry reached his headquarters at the Hotel Merle on St Mark's Place – the other side of the battle area. He had bought the hotel cheap when the Mafia had moved out to Salt Lake City.

Leaving his riders to go to the aid of their comrades on West 4th, he entered the seedy gloom of the lobby.

Shaky Mo Collier was on the desk. His black face was caked with white clay and his expression was unusually surly. He cheered up when he saw Jerry.

"Mornin', guv. Vere's a bloke waitin' fer yer in 506."

"What's his name?"

Mo screwed up his eyes in the poor light and his lips moved as he tried to read something he had scribbled on a checking-in card. "Robin – nar – Reuben – nar – Robert – de – Fate? Nar! Rob..."

"Robert de Fete." Jerry felt relieved. His trip hadn't been wasted. He recognised the "whimsical" pseudonym. "Foreign Office."

Mo sniffed and picked at the clay on his face. "I'll buy it, won' I?"

Jerry chucked him under his chin. "We bought it."

He took the groaning elevator to the fifth floor. The warren of narrow corridors was everywhere painted the same chocolate brown. Jerry found 506.

Cautiously, he opened the door.

The darkened room contained a bed without sheets and blankets. It had a striped, stained mattress. On the floor was a worn green carpet. A bedside table, lamp and secretaire were all coated with several layers of the same brown paint. The blind had been pulled down. On the secretaire stood a half-full bottle of Booth's Gin and a plastic cup.

Jerry opened the door into the bathroom. The pipes gurgled and shook, but the room was empty. He checked the shower-stall just the same.

He went back into the bedroom and looked at the bottle of gin. Obviously, his visitor had left it as a message.

It made sense.

The trip had paid off.

5

The New York Mets moved to within one victory of the pot of gold yesterday when they defeated the Baltimore Orioles 2–1, in 10 innings and took a lead of three games to one in the World Series. The victory was the third straight for the underdog Mets over the champions of the American League and it was laced with potent doses of the "magic" that has marked their fantastic surge to the top in 1969. – *New York Times*, 16 October 1969

Upset or Equilibrium in the Balance of Terror?

Miss Brunner appeared to have cooled down the reversion process somewhat when Jerry returned to the Centre. She was still mumbling, half the doodles on her pads were astrological equations she was either feeding into or receiving from her computer, but the worst part of her work was over now Jerry had isolated the key mark's identity type.

She licked her lips when he handed her the paper with the name on it.

"So it's a morality syndrome?"

"Yes, the poor sod." Jerry rubbed the back of his neck.

"I'll have to take him out as soon as possible. No time for a transmogrification. This'll have to be a termination. Unless . . ." He narrowed his eyes as he looked at her. "Are you sure you're all right?"

"Yes, of course. It's this bloody pattern. You know what it does to me."

"Okay. Well, can you pin him down in a hurry? We had a break in that he's evidently going 'guilty' on us, like a lot of them. They do half our work for us. Very few are ever one hundred per cent sure of themselves. That's why they say they are."

She started to sort through her notes, stopped and picked up a bottle of cologne. She unscrewed the cap, upended the bottle and dabbed some of the cologne on her forehead.

Jerry rocked on the balls of his feet.

"At least it's a familiar pattern," she said. "A standard British resurrection plan of the old type. With 'conscience' overtones. What does Alvarez say?"

Jerry went into the next room. "How's it shaping, Mr Alvarez?"

Alvarez shrugged and spread his hands helplessly. "Most of the Middle East's breaking up. Complete temporal entropy in many areas. It'll be South East Asia next, and you know what that means."

Jerry frowned.

Almost shyly, Alvarez glanced at Jerry. "It's never been this bad, has it, Mr Cornelius?"

Jerry scratched his left hand with his right hand. "How about other sectors?"

Alvarez made a radio call. He listened to the headphones for a while and then swivelled to face Jerry who was now leaning against a console smoking an Upmann Exquisitos.

"Moscow's completely out. New York more or less the same. Half of Peking's down – its southern and western districts. Singapore's completely untouched. No trouble in Shanghai. None in Sydney or Toronto. No trouble in Calcutta, but New Delhi's had it. . ."

Jerry dropped his cigar on the floor and stood on it.

The factor was overplaying his hand.

He went back into Miss Brunner's room and told her the news.

She spoke distantly. "I've got it down to eight localities." She started to tap out a fresh programme and then stopped.

She went to her handbag, picked it up, squatted on the floor of the computing room. She was breathing heavily.

Jerry watched her as she took something from her bag and threw it on the ground. It was a handful of chicken bones. Miss Brunner was casting the runes.

"For God's sake, Miss Brunner!" Jerry took a step towards her. "The whole balance is gone and you're fucking about with bones...."

She raised her head and cackled. "You've got to have faith, Mr C."

"Oh, Christ!"

"Exactly," she mumbled. "It's a sort of progress report on the Second Coming, isn't it? You ought to know after all!"

"Mother of God!"

He pressed the button marked POWER OFF and the computer went dead.

Sometimes he would admit that one form of superstition was as good as another, but he still preferred to rely on the forms he knew. He flung himself on top of Miss Brunner and began to molest her.

They were all operating on instinct at the moment.

Systems Theory and Central Government

Jerry was running.

The backlash was bound to hit London soon and the whole equilibrium would be thrown. Alvarez's dark suggestions about rephasing might have to be implemented. That meant a great deal of work – a long job involving a lot of risks. He wasn't sure he was up to it at the moment.

He would have to play his hunch, picking one locality from the list of eight Miss Brunner had shown him before she reverted.

He ran through a deserted Holland Park. The autumn leaves slapped his face. He headed for the Commonwealth Institute.

Whither ESRO?

The sun had set by the time Jerry arrived outside the Institute where a few lights were burning.

He turned up the collar of his black car coat, walked under the flags, past the pool and into the main hall. It was deserted. He crossed the hall and opened a door at the back. It led into a small corridor. At the end of the corridor was another door. Jerry approached it and read the name on it:

COLONEL MOON

The name seemed right.

Jerry turned the handle of the door. It was unlocked. He walked into absolute blackness.

An electric light went on.

He was in a steel office. There were steel filing cabinets, steel shelves and a steel desk. At the desk sat Colonel Moon, a stiff-backed man, no longer young. A cigarette in a black plastic holder was clamped between his teeth. He had a square, healthy face, a little touched by drink. His eyes were blue and slightly watery. He wore the tweed jacket of a minor Civil Service "poet".

As Jerry entered, Colonel Moon closed a boxfile with one hand. His other hand was still by the light switch on the wall near the desk.

"Miss Brunner is dead, eh? It was just as well, Mr Cornelius. We couldn't have her running wild."

"So you're the Great Terror." Jerry rubbed his left eyelid with his left index finger. He looked casually about. "They don't give you much room."

Moon presented Jerry with a patronising smile. "It serves my simple needs. Won't you sit down?"

Jerry crossed to the far wall and seated himself in the wicker rocker. "Where did you pick this up?"

"Calcutta. Where else?"

Jerry nodded. "I got your message in New York."

"Jolly good."

"I'm not really up to this, but what was it – 'guilt' or something?"

"Sense of fair play, old boy."

Jerry burst out laughing.

"I'll be seeing *you*, Colonel."

6

While the strategic importance of large air-launched weapons declines in the age of ICBMs and submarine-launched ballistic missiles, airborne guided weapons for tactical use grow in importance. Vietnam has become a "testing ground" for a wide range of weapons from the Walleye TV-guided bomb to Bullpup and the radar-homing Shrike. The lessons learned from actual operations are rapidly being applied to new weapons systems such as the AGM-80A Viper and the AGM-79A Blue Eye, both conceived as Bullpup replacements.

– *Flying Review International*, November 1969

Emotion and the Psychologist

In mutable times like these, thought Jerry as he walked into Lionel Himmler's Blue Spot Bar, everything was possible and nothing was likely. His friend Albert the émigré nodded to him from the shadowy corner by the bar, lifting his glass of schnapps in the strobelight, saluting both Jerry and the stripper on the stage.

Jerry flickered to a table, sat down and ordered scotch and milk. Once history ceased to be seen in linear terms, it ceased to be made in linear terms. He glanced at his new watch.

Moon's machinery could be useful if used in conjunction with their own. He was sorry that he'd have to blow up Bhubaneswar, though.

The problems, of course, would be "psychological" rather than "moral" – if "moral" meant what he thought it did. That was, he admitted, one of his blind spots. It was a pity Miss Brunner wasn't herself (or, rather, was too much herself). She had a much better grasp of that sort of thing.

From behind the curtain a record of Mozart's 41st Symphony began to play.

Jerry settled back in his chair and watched the act.

7

Peace rallies drew throngs to the city's streets, parks, campuses and churches yesterday in an outpouring of protest against the Vietnam war. The Times Square area was hit by a colossal traffic jam during rush hour as tens of thousands of demonstrators marched to the culminating event of the day – a rally in Bryant Park, west of the New York Public Library. The park was saturated with people, many of them unable to see the speakers' stand or hear the denunciations of war . . . Mayor Lindsay had decreed a day of mourning. His involvement was bitterly assailed by his political opponents and by many who felt that the nationwide demonstrations were not only embarrassing President Nixon's efforts to negotiate an honorable peace but were giving aid and comfort to the enemy as well. – *New York Times*, 16 October 1969

Technology Review

Miss Brunner would be a complete write-off soon, if she wasn't saved.

She was up to her old tricks. She had constructed a pentagram circuit on the floor of the computer room and she had dug up her goat. It lay in the centre of the pentagram, its liver missing.

Jerry watched for a moment and then closed the door with a sigh. He'd have to deal with Moon himself – and what's more it wouldn't now be a simple take-out.

Moon had known what he was doing when he had arranged events so that Miss Brunner's logic patterns would be scattered. He had doubtless hoped that with Miss Brunner's reversion, the whole Time Centre would be immobilised. It had been a clever move – introducing massive chaos factors into twelve major cities, like that. Moon must have been working on the job a long time.

Now Miss Brunner was doing the only thing she could, under the circumstances.

He turned to Alvarez who was sipping a cup of hot Ribena. "They keep turning up, don't they?"

Alvarez's tone was sardonic. "Will it ever end?"

Westminster Scene

Jerry needed sleep. Miss Brunner could get by on a drop or two of blood at the moment, but it wouldn't do for him. Moon would make a good substitute, of course, if he wasn't now needed as an antidote, but that would anyway mean rushing things, probably buggering them up altogether. It was something of a vicious circle.

He went back to his Ladbroke Grove HQ and took the lift up to the tower where he had his private apartments. He switched on the stereo and soothed himself down with a rather mannered version of Beethoven's Ninth, conducted by von Karajan. He typed his notes on the IBM 2000 and made a hundred copies on his Xerox 3600. It wasn't like the old days, when the Centre had only needed one chronograph and the entire works could be run by a single operator. Perhaps the whole thing should be folded. It was becoming a large randomising feature in its own right.

He followed the Beethoven with a Del Reeves album, after considering a Stones LP. There were some perversions left in the world, but he didn't feel up to that one at present. It would have been like drinking Wild Turkey bourbon in an Austin Princess.

He lay down on the leather ottoman by the window.

He dozed until Alvarez called.

"Absolute Crisis Situation just about to break," Alvarez told him. "I'd say you have three hours. After that, there won't even be a chance of rephasing, if I'm any judge."

"Check," said Jerry and winked at his reflection in the mirror.

Tantaliser

It had to be this way. Jerry couldn't have managed it alone, otherwise. He had been forced to wait for the moment when the feedback would start to hit Moon.

He found him in his office, completely naked, sitting in the middle of a huge and tattered Union Jack, the empty cigarette holder between his teeth. It was the flag that had been missing from the pole Jerry had passed on his way in.

Moon's well-preserved body was pale and knotted with muscle. He was remarkably hairy. He saw Jerry and got up.

"Nice to see you, dear boy. As a matter of interest, how did you find me, originally?"

"Originally? The only person sentimental enough to look after those old outposts was you. I knew you would have left NY. I had a hunch you'd be here."

Moon pursed his lips.

"Coffee?" he said at length. He crossed to a gas-ring set up on one of the steel filing cabinets. He put the kettle on and measured spoonfuls of Camp coffee into orange plastic cups.

"No, thanks," said Jerry.

Moon began to pour the coffee back into the bottle. It flooded over the neck and ran down the sides, staining the label.

"It's a shame you refused to fall back on the old methods," he said. "I thought you would when Miss Brunner went."

"They aren't suitable, in this case," Jerry told him. "Anyway, I've been in a funny mood for some time."

"You've got jolly moralistic all of a sudden, haven't you?" Colonel Moon raised his eyebrows in his "quizzical" expression.

"You shouldn't have done that, Colonel." Jerry began to tremble. "I've never understood the death-wish you people have."

"Ah, well, you see – you're younger than me."

"We'll have to wipe out most of your bloody logic sequence. That's not a 'moralistic' reaction. I'm just annoyed."

Again the "quizzical" expression. "So you say."

Jerry smacked his lips.

"I would have thought," Moon added, "that in your terms my sequence was a fairly simple one."

Jerry couldn't answer. He knew Moon was right.

"Everything's so boringly complicated these days, isn't it?" Moon put his hand on the handle of the kettle and winced. He stiffened his lips and began to pour the water into the cup.

Jerry stopped trembling. He felt quite sympathetic towards Moon now. "It's a question of attitude, I suppose."

Moon looked surprised. There were tears in his eyes; just a few. "Yes, I suppose so."

"Shall we be off?" Jerry removed his black gloves and put

one in each pocket of his car coat. He reached inside the coat, pulling his needler free of its holster.

"Mind if I finish my coffee?"

"I'd appreciate it if you'd hurry up, though." Jerry glanced at his watch. "After all, there's Miss Brunner to think of."

8

Today as an extensive auto trip has confirmed, the only danger along Route 4 is the traffic, which is dreadful, and the potholes, which can shatter an axle. The improved security along the road is one of the more visible examples of the progress achieved over the last year by the allied pacification program. – *New York Times*, 16 October 1969

People

Jerry took Colonel Moon to the basement of the Ladbroke Grove HQ.

The colonel smoothed his iron-grey hair and looked around the bare room. "I thought – well – Miss Brunner?"

"That's next. We're going to have to soften you up a bit first. Jimi Hendrix, I'm afraid."

Jerry went to the hidden panel and opened it. He flipped a toggle switch to turn on the power.

Colonel Moon said: "Couldn't you make it George Formby?"

Jerry thought for a moment and then shook his head. "I'll tell you what. I'll make it early Hendrix."

"Very well. I suppose there isn't much time left. You can't blame me for trying, eh?"

Jerry's eyes were glazed as he waltzed over to Colonel Moon and positioned him. "Time? Trying?"

Colonel Moon put his head in his hands and began to sob.

Jerry took aim with the needler, pulled the trigger. The needles passed through the hands and through the eyes and into the brain. Jerry pulled his little transmogrifier from his pocket and stuck the electrodes on Moon's skull.

Then he switched on the music.

Books

It was *And the Gods Made Love* that did it.

His hands rigid over his eyes, Colonel Moon fell down. He murmured one word: Loyalty. And then was supine.

Jerry reduced the volume and picked up a wrist. It was completely limp.

Thoroughly into it now, Jerry licked his lips, heaved the body on to his back, and left for the Time Centre.

9

ROME, Oct. 15 – Cardinal Cooke, Archbishop of New York, urged the Roman Catholic Synod of Bishops today to consider the present period of "stress and strain" in the church "frankly and positively, with great charity". – *New York Times*, 16 October 1969

He Smashed the "Death Valley" Terror Trap

Jerry stumbled through the door with the body over his shoulder. "All ready. Where's Miss B?"

Alvarez was chewing a beef sandwich. "Still in there. She locked the door a while ago."

"Use the emergency lock to open it, will you?"

"You haven't given yourself much margin." Alvarez spoke accusingly as he operated the lock. The computing room door sank into the floor.

Jerry stepped through. "Close it up again, Mr A."

"Aye, aye, Mr C."

Alvarez was getting very edgy about the whole thing. Jerry wondered if he would have to go.

Blue lights flickered on five points. Red lights, close together, shifted on the far side of the room. The red lights were Miss Brunner's beautiful eyes.

"I've come to help you." Jerry grinned and his teeth felt very sharp.

She screamed.

"Oh, do shut up, Miss B. We're going to break the spell together."

"*BELPHEGOR!*"

"Anything you say."

We Survived the Cave of the 10,000 Crazed Bats

Jerry sucked his lower lip.

Colonel Moon now stood shivering in the centre of the pentagram, an inane grin on his face.

Jerry took the speakers and placed one on each of the five points, then turned the computer to FULL INPUT and switched on the rest of the equipment.

Sparks leapt from point to point and settled into a blue-green flow. It was all very familiar. Colonel Moon's mouth went slack.

"Cheer up, Colonel. You never saw an act like this at the Empire!"

From the darkness, Miss Brunner cackled stupidly.

Jerry turned a dial. The music came out softly at first, but it got to the colonel in no time. It was the Mothers of Invention and *Let's Make the Water Turn Black*.

He heard Miss Brunner through it all. "Tasty," she was saying. At least she was responding a bit.

"In you go, Miss B."

He watched her scrawny, naked body in silhouette as it moved through the blue-green glow into the pentagram.

Colonel Moon hissed as Miss Brunner took her first nip.

Jerry's part of it was over. He slipped from the room.

The antidote had been administered, but there was still a lot of tidying up to do.

Sex Habits of Bonnie Parker and the Women Who Kill

Alvarez was smiling now. He looked up from his headphones. "The situation's static. We've got a silly season on our hands by the smell of it."

Jerry was worn out. "Reset all the chronographs, will you. It's not over yet."

Miss Brunner could be a great asset, but her habits sometimes put him off her.

He yawned. "Poor old Moon."

"Hoist by his own petard, eh?" grinned Alvarez.

"Silly bugger. He didn't really believe in what he was doing."

"But Miss Brunner did."

"Well, Moon felt he ought to have a 'sense of purpose', you see. It lets them all down in the end."

10

It would be foolish to speculate further. – George Steiner

Facts by Request

Miss Brunner and Jerry Cornelius walked hand in hand through Hyde Park and paused where the crater had been.

"It's very hazy," she said. "So I did it again."

"Moon set you up. You knocked him down."

"*C'est la vie!*"

"You could put it like that."

She stopped and removed her hand from his. "Really, Mr Cornelius, you do seem *down*."

"Well, it's all over now. Here's your transport."

He pointed through the trees at the Sikorsky SH-3D which began to rev up, blowing the last of the leaves from the branches, blowing the other leaves up into the air. The day was cold and sunny.

She paused, looking in her handbag for something and not finding it. "You sympathise with them, yet you'll never understand their morality. It was such a long while ago. You're a kind little chap, aren't you?"

Jerry folded his arms and closed his face.

He watched her walk towards the helicopter, her red hair ruffled by the wind. She was full of bounce. Moon had agreed with her.

He thought she called something out, but he couldn't hear her above the whine of the rotors.

The helicopter shuddered and lumbered into the sky.

Soon it was gone.

Jerry looked at his watch. The arrows were revolving at a moderate speed. It was all he could hope for.

The gestures of conflict keep the peace.

It was a motto that even Moon had understood, but he had chosen to ignore it. Those old men of action. They were the ones you had to watch.

Jerry lay down on the grass and closed his eyes. He listened to the lazy sound of the distant traffic, he sniffed the scents of autumn.

It had been a rotten little caper, all in all.

Other texts consulted include:
Real Detective Yearbook, No. 101, 1969
Confidential Detective Cases, March 1969
Women in Crime, May 1969
Male, June 1969
Encounter, August 1969
New Scientist, 13 November 1969

Sea Wolves

Your computer needs you

It occurs to us that while we've been saying "you need your computer" we'd also like to emphasise something equally important.

"Your computer needs you."

You see, without you your computer is nothing.

In fact it's people like yourself that have made the computer what it is today.

It's people like you that have made their computer do some pretty exciting things.

Like help them keep on top of sales trends.

Or design a bridge.

Or keep track of all the parts that go into a giant whirlybird.

To do things like that, your computer needs some help.

It needs you to get more involved with it. So you can use it to help you do more than just the payroll and the billing.

And it needs some terminals.

Terminals let you get information in and out of your computer fast.

They let you get up close to your computer.

Even though you might be miles away . . .

But terminals are nothing unless something happens between you and your computer.

Unless you get involved with your computer.

You need your computer.

Your computer needs you.

KNOW YOUR BUSINESS.
KNOW YOUR COMPUTER.

IBM

1

Running, grinning, aping the movements of the mammals milling about him, Jerry Cornelius made tracks from the menagerie that was My Lai, the monster tourist attraction of the season, and threw his Kamov Ka-15 into the sky, flew over the tops of the tall hotels and novelty factories, away from there; away to the high privacy of Bangkok's Hotel Maxwell where, panting, he froze his limbs in the angles of sleep.

A posture, after all, was a posture.

2

Jerry's uniform was that of the infamous Brigade of St Basil. These Osaka-based White Cossack Mercenaries had recently changed from the Chinese to the American side; a half-hearted move; a compromise. But the uniform – cream, gold and fawn – overrode most other considerations.

Meanwhile revolutionary troops continued to march on the great automated factories of Angkor Wat and Anuradhapura. It would all be over by the Festival of Drakupolo.

A week passed. Jerry continued to sleep, his well-cut jacket and jodhpurs uncrumpled, for he did not stir and his breathing was minimal, neither did he perspire. There was a complete absence of REMs.

3

The war ended with a complete victory for the factories. The defected revolutionaries made their way back to Simla and Ulan Bator. Jerry woke up and listened to the news on Radio Thai. He frowned.

A fine balance had to be maintained between man and machine, just as between man and man, man and woman, man and environment.

It was as good as it was bad.

Regretfully he stripped off his uniform. He was not sure he looked forward to civvy street.

4

The gestures of conflict keep the peace. The descendants of Tompion and Babbage toyed with inaccurate engines while their enemies entertained impossible debates concerning the notion that an electronic calculating device could not possess a "soul". The old arguments perpetuated themselves: resolved in the ancient formulae of warfare.

5

When Jerry arrived in Phnôm Penh the streets were full of bunting. Rickshaws, bicycles, cars and trams were hung with paper banners, streamers and posters. The Central Information Building shuddered with bright flame. The factories had won, but others were suffering for them. It was as it should be, thought Jerry.

Cheerfully he mounted an abandoned British-made Royal Albert gent's black roadster and pedalled along with the procession, avoiding the wreckage of cash-registers and adding machines that had been hurled from shops and offices that morning, heading for the suburbs where his bungalow housed a Leo VII cryogenic storage computer which he had, before the war, been programming on behalf of the monks at the new temple on Kas Rong. But the anti-religious riots had not only been directed at the machines. The monastery had been hastily disbanded by the authorities in the hope that this measure would save the new research wing of the Hospital of the Secret Heart at Chanthaburi. It had not.

6

Jerry entered the bungalow and shivered. The temperature was almost at zero. He pushed back the steel sliding doors of the inner room. The computer glistened under a thick coating of ice.

Was entropy setting in again?

Turning up the collar of his black car coat he inspected the power inputs. Something had overloaded Leo VII.

Jerry sniffed the sharp air. A problem of cardinal importance. He twitched his lips. Time to be moving.

He paused, studying the computer. It trembled under its sheathing of ice. He went to wall and took his kid gloves from his pocket. He pulled them on, pressed the DESTRUCT button, but it would not move. It was frozen solid.

Jerry reached inside his coat and brought out his needle-gun. With the butt he hammered the button home.

He left the computer room. In the living-room ice had formed traceries on the walls and windows, whorls and lines spelling out equations of dubious importance. A little bile came into his throat.

All the signs pointed West.

He went to the garage at the side of the bungalow, wheeled his big BMW 750cc hog on to the path, put it between his legs,

kicked the starter and whisked wild and easy off down the concrete road towards the jungle.

Yellow sun.

Blue sky.

Green trees.

Monkeys screaming.

7

> Zut alors!
> Maxim's in Paris
> buys its fish
> from a machine.

Part of the reason that fish at Maxim's is so fabulous is
because it's so fresh. Fresh from General Electric data-
processing equipment. When a French fisherman unloads his
catch at the port of Sète, a unique data-gathering and display
system takes over . . .

> Progress is our most important product
> GENERAL ELECTRIC

8

A loud shriek.

9

The Dnieper flowed slowly, its muddy waters churned by the
wind. In the brown land some snow remained. The great sky was
low and grey over the steppe. A small wooden landing stage had
moored to it a carved fishing boat, its sail reefed.

On the landing stood three Cossacks. They had long mous-
taches, smoked large pipes, wore big fur caps on the sides of their
shaven heads. Heavy burkas swathed their burly bodies and they

wore baggy trousers of blue or green silk, boots of red or yellow morocco leather. There were sabres at their sides, rifles on their backs. They watched the horseman as he galloped nearer on his shaggy, unshod pony.

The rider had bandoliers of cartridges crossing his chest, an M-60 on his back. He wore the Red Army uniform of the "Razin" 11th Don Cossack Cavalry and he carried the horsehair standard of an ataman. He was young, with long pale hair and sharp blue eyes. He drew his horse to a skidding halt and saluted the three men whose expressions remained set.

"Cossacks of the Zaporozhian Sech, greetings from your brothers of the Don, the Yaik and the Kukan." He spoke with a strong Ukrainian accent, driving the standard into the hard ground.

The nearest Zaporozhian reached down and picked up a sack that lay at his feet. "The Sech is no more," he said. "We and this is all that remains. The great horde came four days ago from the East." He upended the sack and emptied it.

Jerry dismounted and went to stare at the collection of small metal cogs, transistors and tapes.

"The krug is dead." Tears came to the leading Zaporozhian's hard, grey eyes. "The Khan rules. This is the end of our ancient freedom."

Jerry got back on to his horse and rode away. He left the horsehair standard waving in the wind. He left the Cossacks weeping. He left the bank of the muddy Dnieper and headed out across the steppe, riding South again, towards the Black Sea.

10

The anthropomorphic view:

The Bug Slayer

No computer stamps out program bugs like RCA's Octoputer. It boosts programming efficiency up to 40%. Programming is already one-third of computer costs, and going up faster than any other cost in the industry. A lot of that money is eaten up by bugs . . .

11

He wandered along the grassy paths between the ancient ruins. Everywhere was litter. Broken tape-spools crunched beneath his boots, printouts snagged his feet; he was forced to make detours around buckled integrator cabinets. A few white-coated technicians tried to clean up the mess, haul the torn bodies away. They ignored Jerry, who went past them and hit the jungle once more. In his hand he held an ice-pick.

One of the technicians jerked his thumb as Jerry disappeared. "Asesino . . ." he said.

Jerry was glad to be out of Villahermosa.

12

He was cleaning his heat in his hut when the pale young man came in, shut the flimsy door and shuddered. Outside, the jungle stirred.

Jerry replaced rod, rag and oil in their case and carefully closed the lid.

The young man was dressed in a brown tropical suit with sweat-stains under arms and crotch. He had noticed the three weapons in the case: the needler, the heater, the vibragun. He crossed himself.

Jerry nodded and drew on his black leather Norfolk jacket. From the tops of his dark Fry boots he untucked his pink bell-bottomed Levis and smoothed them down with the tips of his fingers, watching the pale young man with amused, moody eyes.

An Aeroflot VC 10 began its approach to the nearby Mowming drome. The windows vibrated shrilly and then subsided.

"The sense of oneness known to the Ancients." The young man waved his hands vaguely in all directions. "At last it is within our grasp."

Jerry rubbed his nose with his case.

"I'm sorry, Mr Cornelius, I am, of course, Cyril Tome." A smile of apologetic patronage. "What a nightmare this world is. But the tide is turning . . ."

Jerry began vigorously to brush his fine blond hair, settling it on his shoulders. "I wasn't expecting you, Mr Tome."

"I left a message. In Kiev."

"I didn't get it."

"You mean you didn't receive it?"

"If you like."

"Mr Cornelius, I gathered from a mutual acquaintance that we were of a similar mind. 'Science is only a more sophisticated form of superstition' – didn't you say that?"

"I'm told so. Who was the acquaintance?"

"Malcolm." He raised his eyebrows. "Beesley? But don't you agree that in place of the old certainties, rooted in the supreme reality of existence, we have transferred our faith to science, the explanation for everything which explains nothing, the ever more fragmented picture of reality which becomes ever more unreal . . ."

"How is Bishop Beesley?"

"Carrying on the fight as best he can. He is very tired."

"He is indeed."

"Then you don't agree . . ."

"It's a question of attitude, Mr Tome." Jerry walked to the washstand and picking up a carton of Swedish milk poured out half a saucer for the half-grown black and white cat which now rubbed itself against his leathered leg. "Still, we don't need emotional rapport, you know, to do business."

"I'm not sure . . ."

"Who is, Mr Tome?"

"I am sure . . ."

"Naturally."

Tome began to pace about the floor of the hut. "These machines. They're inhuman. But so far only the fringes have been touched."

Jerry sat down on the bed again, opening his gun case. He began to fit the vibragun together, snapping the power unit into place.

Tome looked distastefully on. "I suppose one must fight fire with fire."

Jerry picked his teeth with his thumbnail, his brows furrowed. He did not look at Tome.

"What's the pattern?" he murmured, stroking the cat.

"Is there a pattern to anarchy?"

"The clearest of all, I'd have thought." Jerry slipped the vibragun into his shoulder holster. "In Leo VII all things are possible, after all."

"A machine is – "

" – a machine is a machine." Jerry smiled involuntarily.

"I don't understand you."

"That's what I was afraid of."

"Afraid?"

"Fear, Mr Tome. I think we might have to book you."

"But I thought you were on my side."

"Christ! Of course I am. And their side. And all the other sides. Of course I am!"

"But didn't you start the machine riots in Yokohama? When I was there?"

Tome burst into tears.

Jerry rubbed at his face in puzzlement.

"There's been a lot of that."

Tome made for the door. He had started to scream.

Some beastly instinct in Jerry responded to the movement and the sound. His vibragun was slipped from its holster and aimed at Tome as the pale young man fumbled with the catch.

Tome's teeth began to chatter.

He broke up.

All but insensate, Jerry fell back on the bed, his mad eyes staring at the ceiling.

Eventually they cooled.

Jerry left the hut and struck off through the jungle again. He had an overwhelming sense of *déjà vu*.

13

The mechanistic view:

Horace is Hornblower's remarkable new computer system. And what he does with confirmations is a Hornblower exclusive...

Only Horace prints complete confirmations in Seconds

14

Jerry was lost and depressed. Thanks to Tome, Beesley and their fellow spirits, a monstrous diffusion process was taking place.

He stumbled on through the jungle, followed at a safe distance by a cloud of red and blue macaws. They were calling out phrases he could not quite recognise. They seemed malevolent, triumphant.

A man dressed in the tropical kit of an Indian Army NCO emerged from behind a tree. His small eyes were almost as confused as Jerry's.

"Come along, sir. This way. I'll help."

For a moment Jerry prepared to follow the man, then he shook his head. "No, thank you, Corporal Powell, I'll find my own way."

"It's too late for that, Mr Cornelius."

"Nonetheless . . ."

"This jungle's full of natives."

Jerry aimed a shot at the NCO, but the little man scurried into the forest and disappeared.

Several small furry mammals skittered out into the open, blinking red eyes in the direct sunlight. Their tiny thumbs were opposable. Jerry smiled down indulgently.

Around him the Mesozoic foliage whispered in the new, warm wind.

15

He had reached the sea.

He stood on the yellow shore and looked out over the flat, blue water. Irresolutely he stopped as his boots sank into the sand. The sea frightened him. He reached inside his coat and fingered the butt of his gun.

A white yacht was anchoring about a quarter of a mile away.

Soon he heard the sound of a motor-boat as it swept towards him through the surf.

He recognised the yacht as the *Teddy Bear*. It had had several owners, none of them particularly friendly. He turned to run, but he was too weak. He fell down. Seamen jumped from the boat and pulled him aboard.

"Don't worry, son," one of them said. "You'll soon be back in blighty."

"Poor bastard."

Jerry whimpered.

They'd be playing brag for his gear soon.

Because of the sins which ye have committed before God, ye shall be led away captives into Babylon by Nabuchodonosor king of the Babylonians. – *Baruch* 6 : 2

He was feeling sorry for himself. He'd really blown this little scene.

16

Need to improve customer service? Salesman productivity? Here's your answer – Computone's portable computer terminal, the world's smartest briefcase. It weighs only $8\frac{3}{4}$ pounds, and it costs as little as \$20 per month. Through a telephone in the prospect's home or office, your salesman can communicate directly with a computer, enter orders and receive answers to inquiries within seconds. The terminal converts your salesman into a team of experts who bring to the point of sale the vast memory of a computer and its ability to solve problems immediately and accurately. – COMPUTONE SYSTEMS INC. *the company that put the computer in a briefcase*

17

Jerry was dumped outside the Time Centre's Ladbroke Grove HQ. He got up, found his front door, tried to open it. The door was frozen solid. The Leo VII had spread its cryogenic bounty throughout the citadel.

Jerry sighed and leaned against the brick wall. Above his head someone had painted a new slogan in bright orange paint:

NO POPERY

There were only two people who could help him now and neither was particularly sympathetic to him.

Was he being set up for something?

18

Hans Smith of Hampstead, the Last of the Left-wing Intellectuals, was having a party to which Jerry had not been invited.

Because of his interest in the statistics of interracial marriage in Vietnam in the period 1969/70, Hans Smith had not heard about the war. There had been few signs of it on Parliament Hill. Late one night he had seen a fat, long-haired man in a tweed suit urinating against a tree. The man had turned, exposing himself to Smith, grinning and leering. There had also been some trouble with his Smith-Corona. But the incidents seemed unrelated.

Balding, bearded, pot-bellied and very careful, Hans Smith had codified and systemised his sex-life (marital, extra-marital and inter-marital) to the point where most discomfort and enjoyment was excluded. His wife filed his love-letters and typed his replies for him and she kept his bedroom library of pornography and sex-manuals in strict alphabetical order. Instead of pleasure, Smith received what he called "a healthy release". The sexual act itself had been promoted into the same category as a successful operation for severe constipation. Disturbed by the Unpleasant, Smith belonged to a large number of institutions devoted to its extinction. He lived a smooth existence.

Jerry opened the front door with one of the keys from his kit and walked up the stairs. Somewhere The Chants were singing *Progress*.

He was late for the party. Most of the remaining guests had joined their liberal hosts in the bedroom, but Smith, dressed in a red and gold kimono that did much to emphasise the pale obscenity of his body, came to the door at his knock, a vibro-massager clutched in one thin hand. He recognised Jerry and made a Church Army smile through his frown.

"I'm sorry, bah, but . . ."

But Jerry's business was urgent and it was with another guest. "Could I have a word with Bishop Beesley, do you think?"

"I'm not sure he's . . ."

Jerry drew out his heater.

"There's no need to be boorish." Smith backed into the bedroom. Unseen middle-aged flesh made strange, dry sounds. "Bishop. Someone to see you . . ." He fingered his goatee.

Mrs Hans Smith's wail: "Oh, no, Hans. Tell them to fiddle off."

Smith made another of his practised smiles. "It's Cornelius, kitten."

"You said you'd never invite – "

"I didn't, lovie . . ."

Jerry didn't want to look inside, but he moved a step nearer. "Hurry up, Bishop."

Naked but for his gaiters and mitre, the gross white form of Bishop Beesley appeared behind Hans Smith. "What is it?"

"A religious matter, Bishop."

"Ah, in that case." The bishop bundled up his clothes and stepped out. "Well, Mr Cornelius?"

"It's the Leo VII cryogenics. They seem to be trying to convert. I can't make it out. They're freezing up."

"Good God! I'll come at once. A clearing needed, eh? An exorcism?"

Jerry's hunch had been a good one. The bishop had been expecting him. "You'd know better than I, Bishop."

"Yes, yes." Beesley gave Jerry's shoulder a friendly pat.

"Well, the shit's certainly hit the fan," said Jerry. He winked at Smith as he left.

"I'm very glad you called me in, dear boy." Bishop Beesley hopped into his trousers, licking his lips. "Better late than never, eh?"

Jerry shivered.

"It's your baby now, Bishop."

He had another old friend to look up.

19

"One down, eight letters, *To Lucasta, faithful unto death* . . ."
Jerry shrugged and put the newspaper aside. They had arrived. He
tapped the pilot on the shoulder. "Let's descend, Byron."

As the cumbersome Sikorsky shuddered towards the ground,
Jerry had an excellent view of the ruins on the headland. All that
remained of the castle was grass-grown walls a foot or two high,
resembling, from this perspective, a simplified circuit marked out
in stones – a message to an extraterran astronomer. The archaeolo-
gists had been at work again in Tintagel.

Beyond the headland the jade sea boomed, washing the ebony
beach. The Sikorsky hovered over the ocean for a moment before
sweeping backwards and coming to rest near Site B, the monastery.

Dressed in his wire-rimmed Diane Logan black corduroy hat,
a heavy brown Dannimac cord coat, dark orange trousers from
Portugal, and near-black Fry boots, Jerry jumped from the
Sikorsky and walked across the lawn to sit on a wall and watch
the helicopter take off again. He unbuttoned his coat to reveal his
yellow Sachs cord shirt and the Lynn Stuart yellow and black sash
he wore in place of a tie. He was feeling light in his gear but he was
still bothered.

In the hot winter sunshine, he pranced along the footpath that
led to the Computer Research Institute – a series of geodesic domes
stained in bright colours.

"A meaning is a meaning," he sang, "is a meaning is a
meaning."

He was not altogether himself, these days.

Outside the gates he grinned inanely at the guard and displayed his pass. He was waved through.

The Institute was a private establishment. The red moving
pavement took him to the main admin building and the chrome
doors opened to admit him. He stood in the white-tiled lobby.

"Mr Cornelius!"

From a blue door marked DIRECTOR came Miss Brunner,
her auburn hair drawn back in a bun, her stiff body clothed in a
St Laurent tweed suit. She stretched her long fingers at him. He
grasped them.

"And what's your interest in our little establishment, Mr C?" Now she led him into her cool office. "Thinking of giving us a hand?" She studied a tank of small carp.

"I'm not sure I know the exact nature of your research." Jerry glanced around at all the overfilled ashtrays.

She shrugged. "The usual thing. This and that. We're checking analogies at present – mainly forebrain functions. Amazing how similar the human brain is to our more complex machines. They can teach us a lot about people. The little buggers."

He looked at the graphs and charts on her walls. "I see what you mean." He rubbed a weary eye and winced. He had a sty there.

"It's all very precise," she said.

"Get away."

Jerry sighed. Didn't they know there was a war on?

20

"Sweet young stuff," said Miss Brunner. "Tender. Only the best goes into our machines."

Jerry looked at the conveyor, at the aluminium dishes on the belt, at the brains in the dishes.

"They feel nothing," she said, "it's all done by electronics these days."

Jerry watched the battery brains slipping like oysters into the gullets of the storage registers.

"You will try it, won't you?"

"It works both ways," she said defensively.

"I bet it does."

Miss Brunner smiled affectionately. "It's beautifully integrated. Everything automatic. Even the pentagrams are powered."

"This isn't religion," said Jerry, "it's bloody sorcery!"

"I never claimed to be perfect, Mr Cornelius. Besides, compared with my methods the narrow processes of the orthodox . . ."

"You've been driving the whole bloody system crazy, you silly bitch! You and that bastard Beesley. I thought there were only two polarities. And all the while . . ."

"You've been having a bad time, have you? You bloody puritans..."

Jerry pursed his lips. She knew how to reach him.

21

When he got back to Ladbroke Grove he found the door open. It was freezing inside.

"Bishop Beesley?" His voice echoed through the dark passages.

The cold reached his bones.

"Bishop?"

Time was speeding. Perhaps his counter-attack had failed.

He found Beesley in the library. The bishop had never got to the computer. His round, flabby face peered sadly out of the block of ice encasing him. Jerry drew his heater and thawed him out.

Beesley grunted and sat down. "I suppose it was a joke. Doubtful taste..."

"Sorry you were bothered, Bishop..."

"Is that all...?"

"Yes. I must admit I was desperate, but that's over now, for what it was worth."

"You treacherous little oik. I thought you had made a genuine repentance."

Jerry had been triggered off again. His eyes were glowing a deep red now and his lips were curled back over his sharp teeth. His body radiated such heat that the air steamed around it. He waved his gun.

"Shall we press on into the computer room?"

Beesley grumbled but stumbled ahead until they stood before the iced-up Leo VII.

"What point is there in my presence here," Beesley chattered, "when your claims – or its – were plainly insincere?"

"The logic's changed." Jerry's nostrils widened. "We're having a sacrifice instead."

Jerry thought he smelled damp autumn leaves on the air.

He snarled and chuckled and forced the bishop towards the appropriate input.

"Sacrilege!" howled Beesley.

"Sacrosanct!" sniggered Jerry.

Then, with his Fry boot, he kicked Beesley's bottom.

The clergyman yelled, gurgled and disappeared into the machine.

There was a sucking sound, a purr, and almost immediately the ice began to melt.

"It's the price we pay for progress," said Jerry. "Your attitudes, Bishop, not mine, created the situation, after all."

The computer rumbled and began a short printout. Jerry tore it off.

A single word:

TASTY.

22

Like it or not, the Brunner programme had set the tone to the situation, but at least it meant things would calm down for a bit . . . Time to work on a fresh equation.

These alchemical notions were, he would admit, very common-place. The pattern had been begun years before by describing machines in terms of human desires and activities, by describing human behaviour in terms of machines. Now the price of that particular logic escalation was being paid. Beesley had paid it. The sweet young stuff was paying it. The mystical view of science had declined from vague superstition into positive necromancy. The sole purpose of the machines was confined to the raising of dead spirits. The polarities had been the Anthropomorphic View and the Mechanistic View. Now they had merged, producing something even more sinister: the Pathological View.

A machine is a machine is a machine . . . But that was no longer the case. A machine was anything the neurotic imagination desired it to be.

At last the computer had superseded the automobile as the focus for mankind's hopes and fears. It was the death of ancient freedoms.

23

It was raining as Jerry picked his way over the Belgrade bomb-sites followed by crowds of crippled children and the soft, pleading voices of the eleven- and twelve-year-old prostitutes of both sexes.

His clothes were stained and faded. Behind him were the remains of the crashed Sikorsky which had run out of fuel.

On foot he made for Dubrovnik, though a world ruled by bad poets who spoke the rhetoric of tabloid apocrypha and schemed for the fruition of a dozen seedy apocalypses.

At Dubrovnik the corpse-boats were being loaded up. Fuel for the automated factories of Anuradhapura and Angkor Wat. On one of them, if he was lucky, he might obtain a passage East.

Meanwhile machines grew skeletons and were fed with blood and men adopted metal limbs and plastic organs. A synthesis he found unwelcome.

24

Out of the West fled Jerry Cornelius, away from Miss Brunner's morbid Eden, away from warm steel and cool flesh, on a tanker crammed with the dead, to Bombay and from there to the interior, to rest, to wait, to draw breath, to pray for new strength and the resurrection of the Antichrist.

A posture, after all, was a posture.

> You won't make an important decision
> in the 70s without it
> Your own personal desk-top computer
> terminal

Remember the 1970s are just around the corner. A call to Mr A.A. Barnett, Vice President – Marketing, Bunker-Ramo, could be your most important decision for the new decade.

(All ad quotes from *Business Week*, 6 December 1969)

Voortrekker
A Tale of Empire

My Country 'Tis of Thee

Mr Smith said that the new Constitution would take Rhodesia
further along the road of racial separate development –
although he preferred to call it "community development and
provincialisation." He agreed that, initially, this policy would
not improve Rhodesia's chances of international recognition,
but added: "I believe and I sincerely hope that the world is
coming to its senses and that this position will change, that
the free world will wake up to what international communism
is doing." – *Guardian*, 14 April 1970

Think It Over

The group was working and Jerry Cornelius, feeling nostalgic, drew on a stick of tea. He stood in the shadows at the back of the stage, plucking out a basic pattern on his Futurama bass.

"She's the girl in the red blue jeans,
She's the queen of all the teens . . ."

Although The Deep Fix hadn't been together for some time Shaky Mo Collier was in good form. He turned to the console, shifting the mike from his right hand to his left, and gave himself a touch more echo for the refrain. Be-bop-a-lula. Jerry admired the way Mo had his foot twisted just right.

But it was getting cold.

Savouring the old discomfort, Jerry peered into the darkness at the floor where the shapes moved. Outside the first Banning cannon of the evening were beginning to go off. The basement shook.

Jerry's numb fingers muffed a chord. A whiff of entropy.

The sound began to decay. The players blinked at each other. With a graceful, rocking pace Jerry took to his heels.

None too soon. As he climbed into his Silver Cloud he saw the first figure descend the steps to the club. A woman. A flat-foot.

It was happening all over again.

All over again.

He put the car into gear and rippled away. Really, there was hardly any peace. Or was he looking in the wrong places?

London faded.

He was having a thin time and no mistake. He shivered. And turned up the collar of his black car coat.

HOPES FOR U.S. VANISH, he thought. If he wasn't getting older then he wasn't getting any younger, either. He pressed the button and the stereo started playing *Sergeant Pepper*. How soon harmony collapsed. She never stumbles. There was no time left for irony. A Paolozzi screenprint. She likes it like that. Rain fingered his windscreen.

Was it just bad memory?

Apple crumble. Fleeting scene. Streaming screen. Despair.

At the head of that infinitely long black corridor the faceless man was beckoning to him.

Not yet.

But why not?

Would the time ever be right?

He depressed the accelerator.

Diffusion rediffused.

Breaking up baby.

Jump back . . .

He was crying, his hands limp on the wheel as the car went over the ton.

All the old men and children were dying at once.

HANG

ON

"NO!"

Screaming, he pressed his quaking foot right down and flung his hands away from the wheel, stretching his arms along the back of the seat.

It wouldn't take long.

I Love You Because

What the Soviet Union wants in Eastern Europe is peace and quiet . . . – Hungarian editor quoted, *Guardian*, 13 April 1970

Clearwater

"How's the head, Mr Cornelius?"

Miss Brunner's sharp face grinned over him. She snapped her teeth, stroked his cheek with her hard fingers.

He hugged at his body, closed his eyes.

"Just a case of the shakes," she said. "Nothing serious. You've got a long way to go yet."

There was a stale smell in his nostrils. The smell of a dirty needle. Her hands had left his face. His eyes sprang open. He glared suspiciously as she passed the chipped enamel kidney dish to

Shaky Mo who winked sympathetically at him and shrugged. Mo had a grubby white coat over his gear.

Miss Brunner straightened her severe tweed jacket on her hips. "Nothing serious . . ."

It was still cold.

"Brrrr . . ." He shut his mouth.

"What?" She whirled suddenly, green eyes alert.

"Breaking up."

"We've been through too much together."

"Breaking up."

"Nonsense. It all fits." From her large black patent leather satchel she took a paper wallet. She straightened her . . . "Here are your tickets. You'll sail tomorrow on the *Robert D. Fete.*"

Shaky Mo put his head back round the tatty door. The surgery belonged to the last backstreet abortionist in England, a creature of habits. "Any further conclusions, Miss Brunner?"

She tossed her red locks. "Oh, a million. But they can wait."

Heartbreak Hotel

Refugees fleeing from Svey Rieng province speak of increasing violence in Cambodia against the Vietnamese population. Some who have arrived here in the past 24 hours tell stories of eviction and even massacre at the hands of Cambodian soldiers sent from Phnôm Penh. – *Guardian*, 13 April 1970

Midnight Special

The *Robert D. Fete* was wallowing down the Mediterranean coast. She was a clapped out old merchantman and this would be her last voyage. Jerry stood by the greasy rail looking out at a sea of jade and jet.

So he was going back. Not that it made any difference. You always got to the same place in the end.

He remembered the faces of Auchinek and Newman. Their faces were calm now.

Afrika lay ahead. His first stop.

That's When Your Heartaches Begin

Four rockets were fired into the centre of Saigon this evening and, according to first reports, killed at least four people and injured 37.

. . . When used as they are here, in built-up areas, rockets are a psychological rather than a tactical weapon. – *Guardian*, 14 April 1970

Don't Be Cruel

Could the gestures of conflict continue to keep the peace? Was the fire dying in Europe? "Ravaged, at last, by the formless terror called Time, Melniboné fell and newer nations succeeded her: Ilmiora, Sheegoth, Maidahk, S'aaleem. All these came after Melniboné. But none lasted ten thousand years." (The Dreaming City.) In the flames he watched the shape of a teenage girl as she ran about dying. He turned away. Why did the old territorial impulses maintain themselves ("sphere of influence") so far past their time of usefulness? There was no question about it in his mind. The entropy factor was increasing, no matter what he did. The waste didn't matter, but the misery, surprisingly, moved him. Een Schmidt, so Wolenski had said, now had more personal power than Hitler or Mussolini. Was it take-out time again? No need to report back to the Time Centre. The answer, as usual, was written in the hieroglyphs of the landscape. He smiled a rotten smile.

The Facts of Death

"Name your poison, Mr Cornelius."

Jerry raised distant eyes to look into the mad, Boer face of Van Markus, proprietor of the Bloemfontein *Drankie-a-Snel-Snel*. Van Markus had the red, pear-shaped lumps under the eyes, the slow rate of blinking, the flushed neck common to all Afrikaners.

Things were hardening up already. At least for the moment he knew where he was.

"Black velvet," he said. "Easy on the black."

Van Markus grinned and wagged a finger, returning to the bar. "*Skaam jou!*" He took a bottle of Guinness from beneath the counter and half-filled a pint glass. In another glass he added soda water to three fingers of gin. He mixed the two up.

It was eleven o'clock in the morning and the bar was otherwise deserted. Its red flock fleur-de-lis wallpaper was studded with the dusty heads of gnu, hippo, aardvark and warthog. A large fan in the centre of the ceiling rattled rapidly round and round.

Van Markus brought the drink and Jerry paid him, took a sip and crossed to the juke-box to select the new version of *Recessional* sung by the boys of the Reformed Dutch Church School at Heidelberg. Only last week it had toppled The Jo'burg Jazz Flutes' *Cocoa Beans* from number one spot.

> *The tjumelt end the shouwting days;*
> > *The ceptens end the kengs dep'haht:*
> *Stell stends Thine incient secrefize,*
> > *En umble end e contriteart.*
> *Loard Goed ev Osts, be with us yit,*
> > *List we fergit – list we fergit!*

Jerry sighed and checked his watches. He could still make it across Basutoland and reach Bethlehem before nightfall. Originally he had only meant to tank-up here, but it seemed the Republik was running out of the more refined kinds of fuel.

If things went slow then he knew a kopje where he could stay until morning.

Van Markus waved at him as he made for the door.

"Christ, man – I almost forgot."

He rang No Sale on the till and removed something from beneath the cash tray. A grey envelope. Jerry took it, placed it inside his white car coat.

The Silver Cloud was parked opposite the *Drankie-a-Snel-Snel*. Jerry got into the car, closed the door and raised the top. He fingered the envelope, frowning.

On it was written: *Mr Cornelius. The Items.*

He opened it slowly, as a man might defuse a bomb.

A sheet of cheap Russian notepaper with the phrase *Hand in hand with horror: side by side with death* written in green with a felt pen. A place mat from an American restaurant decorated with a map of Vietnam and a short article describing the flora and fauna. Not much of either left, thought Jerry with a smile. A page torn from an English bondage magazine of the mid-50s period. Scrawled on this in black ballpoint: *Love me tender, love me sweet!!!* Although the face of the girl in the picture was half-obscured by her complicated harness, he was almost sure that it was Miss Brunner. A somewhat untypical pose.

The handwriting on envelope, notepaper and picture were all completely different.

Jerry put the items back into the envelope.

They added up to a change of direction. And a warning, too? He wasn't sure.

He opened the glove compartment and removed his box of chessmen – ivory and ebony, made by Tanzanian lepers, and the most beautiful pieces in the world. He took out the slender white king and a delicate black pawn, held them tightly together in his hand.

Which way to switch?

Not Fade Away

SIR: I noticed on page three of the *Post* last week an alleged Monday Club member quoted as follows: "I have listened with increasing boredom to your streams of so-called facts, and I would like to know what you hope to achieve by stirring up people against coloured immigrants."

In order that there should be no doubt whatsoever in the minds of your readers as to the position of the Monday Club in this matter, I would quote from *The New Battle of Britain* on immigration: "Immigration must be drastically reduced and a scheme launched for large-scale voluntary repatriation. The Race Relations Acts are blows against the traditional British right to freedom of expression. They exacerbate rather than lessen racial disharmony. They must be repealed."

In a letter from the Chairman of the Monday Club to

Mr Anthony Barber, Chairman of the Conservative Party, it is stated: "Our fourth finding, and it would be foolish to brush this under the carpet, was that references to immigration were thought to be inadequate. In view of the very deep concern felt about this matter throughout the country, failure to come out courageously in the interests of the indigenous population could threaten the very existence of the party ... However, it was thought there was no good reason to restrict the entry of those people whose forefathers had originally come from these islands ..."

It would be quite wrong to leave anybody with the impression that the Monday Club was not wholly in support of the interests of the indigenous ... population ... of these islands. – D. R. Bramwell (letter to *Kensington Post*, 27 March 1970)

That'll Be The Day

Sebastian Auchinek was a miserable sod, thought Jerry absently as he laid the last brick he would lay for the duration.

Removing his coolie hat he stood back from the half-built wall and looked beyond at the expanse of craters which stretched to the horizon.

All the craters were full of muddy water mixed with defoliants. Not far from his wall a crippled kid in a blue cotton smock was playing in one of the holes.

She gave him a beautiful smile, leaning on her crutch and splashing water at him. Her leg-stump, pink and smooth, moved in a kicking motion.

Smiling back at her Jerry reflected that racialism and imperialism were interdependent but that one could sometimes flourish without the other.

The town had been called Ho Thoung. American destroyers had shelled it all down.

But now, as Jerry walked back towards the camp, it was quiet.

"If the world is to be consumed by horror," Auchinek had told him that morning, "if evil is to sweep the globe and death engulf it, I wish to *be* that horror, that evil, that death. I'll be on the winning side, won't I? Which side are you on?"

Auchinek was a terrible old bit of medieval Europe, really. Doubtless that was why he'd joined the USAF. And yet he was the only prisoner in Ho Thoung Jerry could talk to. Besides, as an ex-dentist, Auchinek had fixed Jerry's teeth better than even the Australian who used to have a surgery in Notting Hill.

Several large tents had been erected amongst the ruins of the town which had had 16,000 citizens and now had about 200. Jerry saw Auchinek emerge from one of these tents, his long body clothed in stained olive drab and his thin, pasty Jewish face as morose as ever. He nodded to Jerry. He was being led to the latrine area by his guard, a boy of fourteen holding a big M60.

Jerry joined Auchinek at the pit and they pissed in it together.

"And how is it out there?" Auchinek asked again. "Any news?"

"Much the same."

Jerry had taken the Trans-Siberian Express from Leningrad to Vladivostok and made the rest of his journey on an old Yugoslavian freighter now owned by the Chinese. It had been the only way to approach the zone.

"Israel?" Auchinek buttoned his faded fly.

"Doing okay. Moving."

"Out or in?"

"A little of both. You know how it goes."

"Natural boundaries." Auchinek accepted a cigarette from his guard as they walked back to the compound. "Vietnam and Korea. The old Manchu Empire. It's the same everywhere."

"Much the same."

"Pathetic. Childlike. Did you get what you came for?"

"I think so."

"Still killing your own thing, I see. Well, well. Keep it up."

"Take it easy." Jerry heard the sound of the Kamov Ka-15's rotors in the cloudy sky. "Here's my transport."

"Thank you," said Auchinek's guard softly. "Each brick brings victory a little closer."

"Sez you."

It's So Easy

"That's quite a knockout, Dr Talbot," agreed Alar. "But how do you draw a parallel between Assyria and America Imperial?"

"There are certain infallible guides. In Toynbeean parlance they're called 'failure of self-determination', 'schism in the body social' and 'schism in the soul'. These phases of course all follow the 'time of troubles', 'universal state' and the 'universal peace'. These latter two, paradoxically, mark every civilization for death when it is apparently at its strongest."

. . . Donnan remained unconvinced. "You long-haired boys are always getting lost in what happened in ancient times. This is here and now – America Imperial, June Sixth, Two Thousand One Hundred Seventy-seven. We got the Indian sign on the world."

Dr Talbot sighed. "I hope to God you're right, Senator."

Juana-Maria said, "If I may interrupt . . ."

The group bowed. – Charles L. Harness. *The Paradox Men*, 1953

Rave On

In Prague he watched while the clocks rang out.

In Havana he studied the foreign liberals fighting each other in the park.

In Calcutta he had a bath.

In Seoul he found his old portable taper and played his late, great Buddy Holly cassettes, but nothing happened.

In Pyongyang he found that his metabolism had slowed so much that he had to take the third fix of the operation a good two months early. Where those two months would come from when he needed them next he had no idea.

When he recovered he saw that his watches were moving at a reasonable rate, but his lips were cold and needed massaging.

In El Paso he began to realise that the alternatives were narrowing down as the situation hardened. He bought himself a second-hand Browning M35 and a new suede-lined belt holster. With ammunition he had to pay $81.50 plus tax. It worked out, as far as he could judge at that moment, to about £1 per person at the current exchange rate. Not particularly cheap, but he didn't have time to shop around.

It Doesn't Matter Any More

It was raining on the grey, deserted dockyard. The warehouses were all boarded up and there were no ships moored any more beneath the rusting cranes. Oily water received the rain. Sodden Heinz and Campbell cartons lurked just above the surface. Broken crates clung to the edge. Save for the sound of the rain there was silence.

Empires came and empires went, thought Jerry.

He sucked a peardrop, raised his wretched face to the sky so that the cold water fell into his eyes. His blue crushed-velvet toreador hipsters were soaked and soiled. His black car coat had a tear in the right vent, a torn pocket, worn elbows. Buttoned tight, it pressed the Browning hard against his hip.

It was natural. It was inevitable. And the children went on burning – sometimes a few, sometimes a lot. He could almost smell them burning.

A figure emerged from an alley between Number Eight and Number Nine sheds and began to walk towards him with a peculiar, rolling, flatfooted gait. He wore a cream trenchcoat and a light brown fedora, light check wide-bottomed trousers with turn-ups, tan shoes. The trenchcoat was tied at the waist with a yellow Paisley scarf. The man had four or five days' beard. It was the man Jerry was waiting for – Sebastian Newman, the dead astronaut.

A week earlier Jerry had watched the last ship steam out of the Port of London. There would be none coming back.

Newman smiled when he saw Jerry. Rotten teeth appeared and were covered up again.

"So you found me at last," Newman said. He felt in the pocket of his coat and came out with a pack of German-made Players. He lit the cigarette with a Zippo. "As they say."

Jerry wasn't elated. It would be a long while before he re-engaged with his old obsessions. Perhaps the time had passed or was still to come. He'd lost even the basic Greenwich bearings. Simple notions of Time, like simple notions of politics, had destroyed many a better man.

"What d'you want out of me?" Newman asked. He sat down on the base of the nearest crane. Jerry leaned against the corrugated door of the shed. There was twenty feet separating them and, although both men spoke quietly, they could easily hear each other.

"I'm not sure," Jerry crunched the last of his peardrop and swallowed it. "I've had a hard trip, Col. Newman. Maybe I'm prepared to give in . . ."

"Cop out?"

"Go for a certainty."

"I thought you only went for outsiders."

"I didn't say that. I've never said that. Do you think this is the Phoney War?"

"Could be."

"I've killed twenty-nine people since El Paso and nothing's happened. That's unusual."

"Is it? These days?"

"What are 'these days'?"

"Since I came back I've never known that. Sorry. That wasn't 'cool', eh?" A little spark came and went in the astronaut's pale eyes.

Jerry tightened his face. "It never stops."

Newman nodded. "You can almost smell them burning, can't you?"

"If this is entropy, I'll try the other."

"Law and order?"

"Why not?"

Newman removed his fedora and scratched his balding head. "Maybe the scientists will come up with something . . ."

He began to laugh when he saw the gun in Jerry's hands. The last 9mm slug left the gun and cordite stank. Newman rose from his seat and bent double, as if convulsed with laughter. He fell smoothly into the filthy water. When Jerry went to look there were no ripples in the oil, but half an orange box was gently rocking.

Bang.

Listen To Me

Europe undertook the leadership of the world with ardor, cynicism and violence. Look at how the shadow of her palaces stretches out ever farther! Every one of her movements has burst the bounds of space and thought. Europe has declined all humility and all modesty; but she has also set her face against all solicitude and all tenderness.

She has only shown herself parsimonious and niggardly where men are concerned; it is only men that she has killed and devoured.

So, my brothers, how is it that we do not understand that we have better things to do than to follow that same Europe?

Come, then, comrades, the European game has finally ended; we must find something different. We today can do everything, so long as we do not imitate Europe, so long as we are not obsessed by the desire to catch up with Europe . . .

Two centuries ago, a former European colony decided to catch up with Europe. It succeeded so well that the United States of America became a monster, in which the taints, the sickness and the inhumanity of Europe have grown to appalling dimensions.

Comrades, have we not other work to do than to create a third Europe? The West saw itself as a spiritual adventure. It is in the name of the spirit, in the name of the spirit of Europe, that Europe has made her encroachments, that she has justified her crimes and legitimized the slavery in which she holds four-fifths of humanity . . .

The Third World today faces Europe like a colossal mass whose aim should be to try to resolve the problems to which Europe has not been able to find the answers . . .
– Frantz Fanon, *The Wretched of the Earth*, 1961

I Forgot to Remember to Forget

The references were all tangled up. But wasn't his job really over? Or had Newman been taken out too soon? Maybe too late. He rode his black Royal Albert gent's roadster bicycle down the hill into Portobello Road. He needed to make better speed than this. He pedalled faster.

The Portobello Road became impassable. It was cluttered by huge piles of garbage, overturned stalls, the corpses of West Indians, Malays, Chinese, Indians, Irish, Hungarians, Cape Coloureds, Poles, Ghanaians, mounds of antiques.

The bike's brakes failed. Jerry left the saddle and flew towards the garbage.

DNA (do not analyse).

As he swam through the stinking air he thought that really he deserved a more up-to-date time machine than that bloody bike. Who was he anyway?

Back to Africa.

Everyday

At the rear of the company of Peuhl knights Jerry Cornelius crossed the border from Chad to Nigeria. The horsemen were retreating over the yellow landscape after their raid on the Foreign Legion garrison at Fort Lamy where they had picked up a good number of grenades. Though they would not normally ride with the Chad National Liberation Front, this time the sense of nostalgia had been too attractive to resist.

Along with their lances, scimitars, fancifully decorated helmets and horse-armour the Peuhl had .303s and belts of ammo crossed over the chainmail which glinted beneath their flowing white surcoats. Dressed like them, and wearing a bird-crested iron helmet painted in blues, reds, yellows and greens, Jerry revealed by his white hands that he was not a Peuhl.

The big Arab horses were coated by the dust of the wilderness and were as tired as their masters. Rocks and scrub stretched on all sides and it would be sunset before they reached the hills and the cavern where they would join their brother knights of the Rey Bouba in Cameroon.

Seigneur Samory, who led the company, turned in his saddle and shouted back. "Better than your old John Ford movies, eh, M. Cornelius?"

"Yes and no." Jerry removed his helmet and wiped his face on his sleeve. "What time is it?"

They both spoke French. They had met in Paris. Samory had had a different name then and had studied Law, doing the odd review for the French edition of *Box Office – Cashiers du Cinema.*

"Exactly? I don't know."

Samory dropped back to ride beside Jerry. His dark eyes glittered in his helmet. "You're always so anxious about the time. It doesn't bother me." He waved his arm to indicate the barren landscape. "My Garamante ancestors protected their huge Saharan empire from the empire of Rome two and a half millennia ago. Then the Sahara became a desert and buried our chariots and our cities, but we fought the Vandals, Byzantium, Arabia, Germany and France."

"And now you're on your way to fight the Federals. A bit of a come down, isn't it?"

"It's something to do."

They were nearing the hills and their shadows stretched away over the crumbling earth.

"You can take our Land Rover to Port Harcourt if you like," Samory told him. The tall Peuhl blew him a kiss through his helmet and went back to the head of the company.

I Love You Because

SIRS: I'm so disgusted with the so-called "American" citizen who knows little or nothing about the Vietnam war yet is so ready to condemn our gov't and soldiers for its actions. Did any of these people that are condemning us ever see their closest friend blown apart by a homemade grenade made by a woman that looks like an "ordinary villager"? Or did they ever see their buddy get shot by a woman or 10-year-old boy carrying a Communist rifle? These people were known VC and Mylai was an NVA and VC village. If I had been there I probably would of killed every one of those goddamned Communists myself. – SP4 Kurt Jacoboni, *Life*, 2 March 1970

I'll Never Let You Go

Sometimes it was quite possible to think that the solution lay in black Africa. Lots of space. Lots of time.

But when he reached Onitsha he was beginning to change his mind. It was night and they were saving on street lighting. He had seen the huts burning all the way from Awka.

A couple of soldiers stopped him at the outskirts of the town but, seeing he was white, waved him on.

They stood on the road listening to the sound of his engine and his laughter as they faded away.

Jerry remembered a line from Camus's *Caligula*, but then he forgot it again.

Moving slowly against the streams of refugees, he arrived in Port Harcourt and found Miss Brunner at the Civil Administration Building. She was taking tiffin with Colonel Ohachi, the local governor, and she was evidently embarrassed by Jerry's dishevelled appearance.

"Really, Mr Cornelius!"

He dusted his white car coat. "So it seems, Miss B. Afternoon, Colonel."

Ohachi glared at him, then told his Ibo houseboy to fetch another cup.

"It's happening all over again, I see." Jerry indicated the street outside.

"That's a matter of opinion, Captain Cornelius."

The colonel clapped his hands.

Can't Believe You Wanna Leave

Calcutta has had a pretty rough ride in the past twelve months and at the moment everyone is wondering just where the hell it goes from here. There aren't many foreigners who would allow the possibility of movement in any other direction. And, in truth, the problems of Calcutta, compounded by its recent vicious politics, are still of such a towering order as to defeat imagination; you have to sit for a little while in the middle of them to grasp what it is to have a great city and its seven million people tottering on the brink of disaster. But that is the vital point about Calcutta. It has been tottering for the best part of a generation now, but it hasn't yet fallen. – *Guardian*, 14 April 1970

True Love Ways

"I thought you were in Rumania," she said. "Are you off schedule or what?"

She came right into the room and locked the door behind her. She watched him through the mosquito netting.

He smoked the last of his Nat Sherman's Queen-Size brown Cigarettellos. There was nothing like them. There would be nothing like them again.

She wrinkled her nose. "What's that bloody smell?"

He put the cigarette in the ashtray and sighed, moving over to his own half of the bed and watching her undress. She was all silk and rubber and trick underwear. He reached under the pillow and drew out what he had found there. It was a necklace of dried human ears.

"Where did you get this?"

"Jealous?" She turned, saw it, shrugged. "Not mine. It belonged to a GI."

"Where is he now?"

Her smile was juicy. "He just passed through."

I Want You, I Need You, I Love You

"Relying on U.S. imperialism as its prop and working hand in glove with it, Japanese militarism is vainly trying to realize its old dream of a 'Greater East Asia Co-Prosperity Sphere' and has openly embarked on the road of aggression against the people of Asia." – Communiqué issued jointly from Chou-en-Lai and Kim-il-Sung (President of North Korea) quoted in *Newsweek*, 20 April 1970

Maybe Baby

Jerry's colour vision was shot. Everything was in black and white when he arrived in Wencslaslas Square and studied the fading wreaths which lay by the monument. Well-dressed Czechs moved about with brief-cases under their arms. Some got into cars. Others boarded trams. It was like watching a film.

He was disturbed by the fact that he could feel and smell the objects he saw. He blinked rapidly but it didn't help.

He wasn't quite sure why he had come back to Prague. Maybe he was looking for peace. Prague was peaceful.

He turned in the direction of the Hotel Esplanade.

He realised that Law and Order were not particularly compatible.

But where did he go from here?

And why was he crying?

It's So Easy

Weeping parents gathered in the hospital and mortuary of the Nile Delta farming towns of Huseiniya last night as Egypt denounced Israel for an air attack in which 30 children died. The bombs were reported to have fallen on a primary school at Bahr el Bakar, nearby, shortly after lessons had begun for the day. A teacher also died, and 40 children were injured.

In Tel-Aviv, however, the Israeli Defence Minister, General Dayan, accused Egypt of causing the children's deaths by putting them inside an Egyptian army base. The installations hit, he said, were definitely military. "If the Egyptians installed classrooms inside a military installation, this, in my opinion, is highly irresponsible." – Guardian, 9 April 1970

All Shook Up

Back to Dubrovnik, where the corpse-boats left from. As he waited in his hotel room he looked out of the window at the festering night. At least some things were consistent. Down by the *docks they were loading the bodies of the White South Afrikan cricket team. Victims of history? Or was history their victim? His nostalgia for the fifties was as artificial as his boyish nostalgia, in the fifties, for the twenties.*

What was going on?

Time was the enemy of identity.

Peggy Sue Got Married

Jerry was in Guatemala City when Auchinek came in at the head of his People's Liberation Army, his tanned face sticking out of the top of a Scammel light-armoured car. The sun hurt Jerry's eyes as he stared.

Auchinek left the car like toothpaste from a tube. He slid down the side and stood with his Thompson in his hand while the photographers took his picture. He was grinning.

He saw Jerry and danced towards him.

"We did it!"

"You changed sides?"

"You must be joking."

The troops spread out along the avenues and into the plazas, clearing up the last of the government troops and their American advisers. Machine guns sniggered.

"Where can I get a drink?" Auchinek slung his Thompson behind him.

Jerry nodded his head back in the direction of the pension he had been staying in. "They've got a cantina."

Auchinek walked into the gloom, reached over the bar and took two bottles of Ballantine from the cold shelf. He offered one to Jerry who shook his head.

"Free beer for all the workers." The thin Jew broke the top off the bottles and poured their contents into a large schooner. "Where's the service around here?"

"Dead," said Jerry. "It was fucking peaceful . . ." Warily, Jerry touched his lower lip.

Auchinek drew his dark brows together, opened his own lips and grinned. "You can't stay in the middle forever. Join up with me. Maxwell's boys are with us now." He looked at the bar mirror and adjusted his Che-style beret, stroked his thin beard. "Oh, that's nice."

Jerry couldn't help sharing his laughter. "It's time I got back to Ladbroke Grove, though," he said.

"You used to be a fun lover."

Jerry glanced at the broken beer bottles. "I know."

Auchinek saluted him with the schooner. "Death to Life, eh? Remember?"

"I didn't know this would happen. The whole shitty fabric in tatters. Still, at least you've cheered up . . ."

"For crying out loud!" Auchinek drank down his beer and wiped the foam from his moustache. "Whatever else you do, don't get dull. Jerry!"

Jerry heard the retreating forces' boobytraps begin to go off. Dust drifted through the door and swirled in the cone of sunlight. Miss Brunner followed it in. She was wearing her stylish battle-dress.

"Revolution, Mr Cornelius! 'Get with it, kiddo!' What do you think?" She stretched her arms and twirled. "It's all the rage."

"Oh, Jesus!"

Helpless with mirth, Jerry accepted the glass Auchinek put in his hand and, spluttering, tried to swallow the aquavit.

"Give him your gun, Herr Auchinek." Miss Brunner patted him on the back and slid her hands down his thighs. Jerry fired a burst into the ceiling.

They were all laughing now.

Any Way You Want Me

Thirty heads with thirty holes and God knew how many hours or minutes or seconds. The groaning old hovercraft dropped him off at Folkestone and he made his way back to London in an abandoned Ford Popular. Nothing had changed.

Black smoke hung over London, drifting across a red sun.

Time was petering out.

When you thought about it, things weren't too bad.

Oh, Boy

He walked down the steps into the club. A couple of cleaners were mopping the floor and the group was tuning up on the stage.

Shaky Mo grinned at him, hefted the Futurama. "Good to see you back in one piece, Mr C."

Jerry took the bass. He put his head through the strap.

"Cheer up, Mr C. It's not the end of the world. Maybe nothing's real."

"I'm not sure it's as simple as that." He screwed the volume control to maximum. He could still smell the kids. He plucked a simple progression. Everything was drowned. He saw that Mo had begun to sing.

The 1500 watt amp roared and rocked. The drummer leaned over his kit and offered Jerry the roll of charge. Jerry accepted it, took a deep drag.

He began to build up the feedback.

That was life.

Other references:
Buddy Holly's Greatest Hits (Coral)
This is James Brown (Polydor)
Elvis's Golden Records (RCA)
Little Richard All-time Hits (Specialty)

Dead Singers

"It's the old-fashioned Time Machine method again, I'm afraid." Bishop Beesley snorted a little sugar, gasped, grinned, put the spoon back in the jade box and tucked the box into the rich folds of his surplice. "Shoot."

"Shot," said Jerry reminiscently. He was really in the shit this time. He plucked the used needle from his left forearm and looked intently at the marks. He rolled down his white sleeve. He pulled on the old black car coat.

Rubbing his monstrous belly, Beesley pursed his little lips. "I've never appreciated your humour, Mr Cornelius. Like it or not, you're tripping into the future. Where, I might add, you richly belong."

Jerry rolled his eyes. "What?"

"That's all in the past now." Beesley waddled to the other side of the tiled room and wheeled the black Royal Albert gent's roadster across the clean floor. He paused to flip a switch on the wall. *Belly Button Window* flooded through the sound system. They were turning his own rituals against him. Now the devil had all the songs.

"All aboard, Mr C."

Reluctantly, Jerry mounted the bike. He was getting a bit too old for this sort of thing.

To the people living in it, no matter how "bad" it might seem by different standards, thought Jerry as he pedalled casually along the Brighton seafront, the future will have its ups and downs. Not too good, not too bad. Society isn't destroyed; it merely alters. Different superstitions; different rituals. We get by. And (he avoided the dead old lady with the missing liver who lay in the middle of the road) we make the rules to fit the situation. He turned up Station Road, pedalling hard. Mind you, you couldn't escape the fucking smell. Oh, Jesus! Nowadays all the fish were frozen.

Faithful to the bishop's briefing, Jerry was doing his best to hate the future, but he'd lived with it too long. A series of useful small events always prepared you for the main one. Soldiers in Bogside prepared the way for soldiers in Clydeside and martial law. Shooting prisoners at Attica made it easier to shoot strikers in Detroit. So you got used to it. And when you were used to it, it wasn't so bad. He cycled past the burnt out remains of the Unicorn Bookshop, an early casualty of the Brighton Revival. Who was invoking what, for Christ's sake? One man's future was another man's present.

The dangers were becoming evident. It was cold and still. Entropy had set in with a vengeance. He carefully stowed the bike on the back seats of the Mercedes G4/W31. The bike was his only real transport. He started the convertible's 5401-cc engine and rolled away past the Pavilion making it into the South Downs where the seeds of the disaster had been sown all those years ago. Rural thinking; rural living. His only consolation was that the Rats had got the cottage-dwellers first.

When the Screamers had finally turned on Lord Longford and cast him forth after he'd dared voice the mildest suggestion that perhaps things were going just a trifle too far in some directions, a sweet-faced, mad-eyed girl had a vision which proved Longford had been the Antichrist all along. The circumstances surrounding his death, two weeks later, remained mysterious, but the event itself improved morale tremendously amongst his ex-followers. At the following Saturday's book-burning in Hyde Park observers had noted a surge of fresh enthusiasm.

A death or two would do it every time.

Jerry had decided not to resign from the Committee, after all. But now the job was done; the ball had rolled. It was peaceful at last. A wind hissed through the wasted hills. Jerry wondered what had happened to his own family. But there wasn't time for that. He kept going. It was getting colder.

The turning point must have been in the Spring of 1970. Given a slightly different set of circumstances, it should have been nothing more than the last death-kick of the Old Guard and everything would have been okay. But somehow the thing had gathered impetus. By Spring 1972 he realised the Phoney War had become a shooting war. Maybe Lobkowitz had been right when they'd last met in Prague. "The war, Jerry, is endless. All we can ever reasonably hope for are a few periods of relative peace. A lull in the battle, as it were." Just as the middle-class "liberals" and "radicals" had got the Attica rebels ready for the massacre, so they had set up British workers for the chop. The final joke of the dying middle class. Lawyers, managers, TV producers and left-wing journalists: they had been the real enemy. Still, it was too late in 1967 to start worrying about that and it was certainly too late now. If, of course, it *was* now. He was feeling a bit vague. Images flickered on the windscreen. A fat, middle-aged woman in a cheap pink suit ran a few yards in front of him and vanished. She reappeared where she had started and did it all over again. She kept doing it. He was losing any cool he'd thought he had.

"Shit."

From the sky he heard Jefferson Airplane. It was all distorted, but it seemed to be *War Movie*. Someone was trying to reach him, and halfway down Croydon High Road at that. Some misguided friend who didn't realise that that sort of thing couldn't possibly work here. The buildings on either side of him were tall, burnt out and crazy, but it was still Saturday afternoon. The ragged people traipsed up and down the pavements with their empty shopping bags in their hands, looking for something to buy. A few Rats in a jeep cruised past them, but the Rats were too interested in Jerry's Mercedes to do anything about the shoppers. Jerry reached into the back and grasped the crossbar of the Royal Albert. The scene was slicing up somewhat. He heard a shout from a roof. A woman in a black leather trenchcoat was shouting to him from the top of Kennard's Department Store. She was waving an M16 in each hand.

"Jerry!" There was some nasty echo there. "Jerry!"

It could have been anyone. He put his foot down on the accelerator and got moving. Speed could do nothing but worsen this frozen situation. There again, he'd no other choice.

In London he slowed down, but by that time he'd blown it completely. Still, he'd got what Beesley wanted. Nothing stayed the same. Tiny snatches of music came from all sides, trying to take hold. Marie Lloyd, Harry Champion, George Formby, Noël Coward, Cole Porter, Billie Holliday, MJQ, Buddy Holly, The Beatles, Jimi Hendrix and Hawkwind. He hung on to Hawkwind, turning the car back and forth to try to home in, but then it was Gertrude Lawrence and then it was Tom Jones and then it was Cliff Richard and he knew he was absolutely lost. Buildings rose and fell like waves. Horses, trams and buses faded through each other. People grew and decayed. There were too many ghosts in the future. In Piccadilly Circus he brought the Mercedes to a bumping stop at the base of the Eros statue and, grabbing the Royal Albert, threw himself clear. He was screaming for help. They'd been fools to fuck about with Time again. Yet they'd known what they were getting him into.

Bishop Beesley stood looking down at him. The bishop had one foot in Green Park, one foot resting on the roof of the

Athenaeum. His voice was huge and distant. "Well, Mr Cornelius, what did you find?"

Jerry whimpered.

"If you want to come back, you'll have to have some information with you."

Jerry pulled himself together long enough to say: "I've got some."

He stood in the clean, tiled room. The Royal Albert was scratched and rusty. Its tyres were flat. It had taken as bad a beating as he had. Munching a Mars, Bishop Beesley leaned against the steel door which opened onto the street.

"Well?"

Jerry dropped the bike to the floor and stumbled up to him, trying to push past, but the bishop was too heavy. He was immovable. "Well?"

"It's what you wanted to know." Jerry looked miserably at the shit on his boots. "The cleanup succeeded. All the singers are dead."

Bishop Beesley smiled and opened the door to let him into Ladbroke Grove. He went out of a house he had once thought was his own. "Bye, bye, now, Mr C. Don't do anything I couldn't do."

The cold got to Jerry's chest. He began to cough. As he trudged along the silent street in the grey autumn evening, the birds stood on their branches and window-ledges, shifting from foot to foot so that their little chains chinked in the staples. They didn't take their unblinking eyes off him. As Jerry turned up the collar of his threadbare coat he had to smile.

The Longford Cup

The following narrative appears to be incomplete. It was discovered in the fireplace of a ruined convent in London's so-called Forbidden Sector. It is largely a record of conversations held by the notorious criminal Cornelius and some of his associates during the period shortly before and immediately during the Re-affirmation of Human Dignity. It is published for the Committee alone. It is imperative that it be in no manner whatsoever made public. The notes were probably compiled by one of our special workers (several of whom came to be on terms of intimacy with Cornelius and, as the Committee already knows from Report PTE5, are still missing). We regret that much of the narrative is likely to distress members of the Committee but present it un-edited so that they may exactly understand the depths of depravity to which persons such as Cornelius had sunk before the Re-affirmation. We have retained the original title – which doubtless refers to our former President – though we recognise that it is obscure. We have numbered the items. Cornelius is believed to be still at large and it is likely that extra efforts will be needed before he can be apprehended. – MEW.

1

"Nothing in my work points to any impulse to develop hostility to the sexual deviant, homosexual, or 'gay' individual – whatever one may call them. But is obvious from the way in which one's work on these problems is received (and often suppressed), that there is a kind of freemasonry in the background, by which those with bizarre sexual tastes are trying to censor debate. This is dangerous . . ." David Holbrook in a letter to the *Guardian*, 28 September 1972

2

"Well, the rich are getting richer and the poor are getting poorer, Mr C." Shaky Mo Collier held the door of the Phantom VII while Jerry stepped, blinking, out. Mo's long greasy hair emerged from under an off-white chauffeur's cap and spread over the shoulders of his grubby white uniform jacket. Mo was looking decidedly seedy, as if the brown rice and Mandrax diet Jerry had recommended wasn't doing him all the good it should.

Jerry smoothed the pleats of his blue midi-skirt and ran the tips of his fingers under the bottom of his fawn Jaeger sweater. He looked every inch the efficient PA. There were auburn highlights in his well-groomed shoulder-length coiffure and the long chiffon scarf tied at his throat, coupled with the neatly overdone make-up, gave him the slight whorish look that every girl finds useful in business. Opening a tooled leather shoulder bag he looked himself over in the flap mirror. He winked a subtly mascara'd eye and offered Mo a jolly grin.

"Cor!" said Mo admiringly. "You little yummy."

Jerry stepped through the glass doors and into the foyer, his pleats swinging to just the right tempo.

In the lift he met Mr Drake from Publicity.

"It must be a heavy responsibility," said Mr Drake. His pallor was at odds with his thick, red lips. He fingered his green silk tie and left a tiny sweat stain near the knot. "Working for such a busy and influential man. Doesn't it ever get on top of you? How does he fit it all in?"

"It's a question of technique really," said Jerry. He giggled. The doors opened.

"See you," said Mr Drake. "Be good."

Jerry stepped along the corridor.

This particular job was beginning to get dull. He'd never been fond of undercover work. Besides, he had the information now. The crucial decision had come at the last full meeting of the Committee (Jerry had been taking the minutes) when it had been agreed, in the words of Jerry's boss, to "use the devil's own troops against him". Files on the sexual preferences of people in high places had been compiled. In return for the original copies of their files they had to give their active help in the campaign. It was surprising how smoothly the method worked already. The police in particular, who had once been able to control and profit from the distribution of erotica, had been only too pleased to see a return to the old *status quo*. Everything and everyone was settling back nicely, by and large. Even the taste for the stuff was a pre-'70s habit.

At the end of this week, Jerry decided, he would give his notice.

He walked through the oak door and into the untidy office. His employer, who almost aways got in early, beamed at him. "There you are, my dear." He rose from behind the desk, putting his ugly fingers to the top of his bald head and with his other hand gesturing towards his visitor.

The visitor – in clerical frock-coat and gaiters – took up a lot of space. Flipping through a piece of research material, he had his huge back to Jerry, but he was immediately identifiable.

"This is Bishop Beesley. He is to take poor Mr Tome's place on the Committee."

The bishop slowly presented his front, like an airship manoeuvring to dock, his jowls shaking with the effort of his smile. It was impossible for Jerry to tell from the expression in the tiny twinkling eyes if he had, in turn, been recognised by his old enemy.

"My dear." Beesley's voice was as warm and thick as butterscotch sauce.

"Bishop." Jerry let his lips part a fraction. "Welcome aboard. Well . . ." He continued towards his own office on the far side of the desk.

"Allow me," Bishop Beesley lumbered to the door and opened it for Jerry.

That was what the power struggle was all about really, thought Jerry as, with a graceful smile, he swept past. He could almost feel the bishop's hand on his bottom.

3

A revival of the '50s sexual aesthetic had never been that far away. How swiftly people recoiled from even a hint of freedom. Lying amidst the tangled sheets Jerry watched as Miss Brunner togged herself up in her stockings, her suspenders, her chains. She had an awful lot in common with Bishop Beesley. Jerry frowned, considering a new idea. Using the last of his Nepalese, he rolled himself a fat joint. He began to drift. Even he could understand the sense of relief she must have. His own girdle hung on the chair to his right.

Her voice was controlled and malicious as she tugged the zip of the black silk sheath dress, a Balenciaga copy. "That's much better, isn't it?" Gazing savagely into the mirror, she began to brush her dark red hair.

"Comfortable?" Jerry offered her the joint.

She shook her head and picked up an atomiser. The room became filled with *Mon Plaisir*. Jerry reeled.

"Maybe I should get myself one of those Ted suits?" he said. "What else? A fancy waistcoat. A yellow Paisley cravat?" His memory was poor on the details. "Crêpes?"

Miss Brunner was disapproving. She bent to powder her nose. "I don't think you really understand, Mr Cornelius."

He reached for another pillow. Propping it behind him he sat up. "I think I do. The cards had already been punched. What's happening was inevitable. Is there a safer bolt-hole than the plastic '50s?"

"Some people take these things seriously." Her face was now a mask of moral outrage. "You talk of fashion while I speak of morality."

It was true that Jerry had never been able to see much of a difference between the two.

"But the clothes . . .?" he began. "All this tight gear."

"They make me feel dignified."

Jerry's laughter was amazed and coarse. "Well," he said. "Fuck that."

"A typical masculine reaction." She put the lipstick to her mouth.

"You should know."

It was obviously time to go home and look up the family.

4

Mrs Cornelius waddled to the door at Jerry's knock. He saw her coming through the cracked and dirty glass. He had had a haircut and a shave and was wearing a nice blue suit. She unbolted the door.

"Hello, Mum."

"Blimey! Look who it isn't!" Her red face was almost the exact match to her dirty dress. Blowsy as ever, she was disconcerted, pushing her stiff peroxide locks back from her forehead. Then she guffawed. "Cor! 'Ullo, stranger." She called back into the dank darkness of her home. "Caf! Wot a turn up! It's yer brother!"

As she closed and locked the door behind Jerry she added: "This we got ter celebrate!"

In the kitchen Jerry saw his sister Catherine. She was looking pale but beautiful, her blonde hair in a score of tiny braids. She was wearing a blue and white Moroccan dress from under which her beaded sandals poked. The room itself was in its usual state, disordered and decrepit, with piles of old newspapers and magazines on every surface.

"I didn't know you were living here, Cathy," he said.

"I'm not. I just dropped in to see Mum. How are things with you, then?"

"Up and down." He selected a relatively safe chair, removed about thirty copies of *Woman* and *Woman's Own* and seated himself opposite her at the table while their mother rummaged in the warped sideboard for a quarter-bottle of gin.

"Yore lookin' nice." Mrs Cornelius found the gin and unscrewed the cap, pouring half the bottle into a cup, offering the rest vaguely, knowing they would refuse. "More than I can say for 'er – all dressed up like a bleedin' wog. I bin tellin' 'er – she thought she was pregnant – 'ow can she be bloody pregnant, 'angin' rahnd with a lot of long-'aired nanas? One thing she *don't* 'ave ter worry abaht – gettin' pregnant off of one of them bloody 'ippies. I said – wait till yer find yerself a *real* man – then yer'll be up the stick fast enough."

"Mum!" Catherine's protest was mild and automatic. She hadn't really been listening.

Mrs Cornelius sniffed. "I'm not sayin' anything was different in my day – we all 'ave ter 'ave our fun – but in my day we didn't bloody go on abaht it all the time. Kept ourselves to ourselves."

"It was the middle-classes finding out." Jerry winked at his sister. "They had to shout it all over the street, eh, Mum?"

"Dunno wot yer talkin' abaht." She smiled as the gin improved her spirits.

"What did they all do before they discovered sex?" Jerry wondered.

"Pictures and dancing," said Catherine, "to Ambrose and his Orchestra. It was the war buggered that. That's how they found out. But it took them till 1965 before it really hit them. Now they've gone and spoiled it for the rest of us. Trust the bloody BBC."

Mrs Cornelius glared stupidly at her children, feeling she was being deliberately excluded.

"Well," she said brutally, "it's love what makes the world go rahnd." With an air of studied reminiscence she reached out and began to finger a tarnished gilt model of the Eiffel Tower. "Paris in the spring," she said. She was referring to her favourite and most familiar love affair. Presumably it had been with Jerry's father, but she had always been unclear on that particular detail of the story, though her children knew everything else by heart.

"There *was* more romance then." Catherine seemed genuinely regretful. Jerry found himself loving them both. He tried to think of something comforting to say.

"We're trying to find our moral and sexual balance at present, maybe," he said. "Things will sort themselves out in time. Meanwhile the old apes drape themselves in wigs and gowns and mortarboards and play at judges and scholars, gnashing their yellow fangs, wagging their paws, scampering agitatedly about. Wasted Longford, lost Muggeridge and melancholy Mrs W. Somewhere you can hear them whimpering, as if the evidence of their own mortality were emphasised by the knowledge of other people's happiness."

They stared at him in astonishment.

He blushed.

5

"Bugger me!" said Shaky Mo. He leaned against the Phantom VII, his jacket open to reveal the purple Crumb tee-shirt covering his underprivileged chest. Jerry sat on the far side of the garage, working at the bench, checking his heat. He wore heavy shades, a long skirted jacket of black kid, black flared trousers and black high-heeled cowboy boots with yellow decorative stitching. The buckle of his wide plaited-leather belt must have measured at least six inches across; it was solid brass. "Well, bugger me. What are we up to now, Mr C?"

Jerry smeared grease on his needle-gun. He checked the action and was happy.

"Nice one," said Mo.

Jerry grinned. His sharp teeth gleamed. His movements were fast and neat as he tucked the gun into its shoulder holster.

"Things are speeding up again, Mo."

Jerry got into the back of the car and stretched out with a satisfied sigh. Mo leapt happily into the driving seat and started the engine.

"It's always a relief when tenderness transmutes into violence." said Jerry.

"Not that violence is without its responsibilities, too. But it's so much easier."

Mo, on the other side of the glass partition, didn't hear a word.

Jerry got a flash then. The dope was making him silly. He shrugged "We can't all be perfect."

6

Miss Brunner looked him over admiringly, "That's more like it. That's what I call a man."

Jerry sneered.

At this an expression of adoration swiftly came and went in her eyes. She moved greedily towards him, touching his belt buckle, stroking his jacket, fingering the pearl buttons of his shirt.

"Oh, what slaves we are to fashion, after all!"

"Glad to be back in the game." Jerry's hand was on her neck, touching filmy fabric, soft skin, delicate hair. "When's Beesley due?"

"Any minute. But I could stall him." Her lips trembled.

Jerry removed his hand. "We'll save that up for the celebration."

Her flat was luxurious, with white fluffy carpets, deep armchairs, lots of multi-coloured cushions, pleasant prints on the pale walls; the sort of hide-out any tired businessman would have welcomed.

There was a knock on the door of this nest. Jerry crossed the carpet and entered the bedroom. He heard Bishop Beesley's muffled voice, a parody of courtliness.

"Your adoring servant, dear lady, I have only an hour. The Committee calls. But how better to spend an hour than in the company of the most beautiful, the *sweetest* woman in London?"

"What a flatterer you are, Bishop!" Her voice was a mixture of vanity and contempt. Jerry, who was having trouble sustaining his rôle, felt deeply sorry for her. As usual when his tenderness and his love were aroused, his head became filled with a variety of pompous and speciously philosophical observations. He controlled himself, promising that he would indulge all that later. Standing with his back to her fitted wardrobe he could see himself in the mirror of her kidney-shaped dressing-table, his hair hanging long and straight and black, his shades glinting. The mirror helped him resume his proper attitude of mind. He snarled at himself.

Miss Brunner entered the bedroom, calling back: "With you in a second, Bishop."

She had known that he would follow. He heaved his huge body after her, beaming affectionately, his fat little hands outstretched to touch her.

"A kiss, dear lady. A token . . ." He shivered. His red lips blubbered. His hot eyes were damp with anticipation. "After last night I would – you could – oh, I am yours, dear lady. Yours!"

Miss Brunner's laughter was perhaps not as harsh as she would have liked. Indeed, there was something of a quaver in it.

"Pig," she said.

It did not have quite the expected effect. He fell to his fat knees. "And sinner, too," he agreed. He buried his head in her thighs, his saliva gleamed on the black silk, he threatened her balance; she almost fell. She clutched at the tufts of hair on both sides of his head and steadied herself.

"Yes!" he groaned. "Yes!"

Jerry had began to enjoy the scene so much (including Miss Brunner's discomfort) that he was reluctant to act; but he pulled himself together, gave his reflection a parting snarl, and moved round the bed.

"Bishop."

Beesley paused, drew back a fraction and stared enquiringly up into Miss Brunner's unhappy face.

She cleared her throat. "I'm afraid we are discovered, Bishop."

Beesley considered this. Then, with a certain amount of studied dignity, he got to his feet, his back still towards Jerry. He turned.

"Afternoon, Bishop," said Jerry. "So much for the sanctity of the home, eh?"

Beesley looked hopefully at Miss Brunner.

"My husband," she explained.

"Cornelius?" Beesley was indignant. "You hate him. You can't stand him. You told me so. Not your type at all."

"He does have his off days," she agreed.

"The fact remains," said Jerry. "You ought to know what marriage means, Bishop. After all, you're a married man yourself."

"You intend to blackmail me?" Now that he felt he understood their motives Bishop Beesley relaxed a trifle.

"Of course not." Jerry slipped his needle-gun from its holster. "It's time you got undressed. Isn't that what you came for?"

7

Afterwards, while Bishop Beesley lay grunting in uncomfortable slumber on the edge of the rug, Jerry stretched himself fully clothed beside Miss Brunner's wet, warm and naked body. He put an arm round her triumphant shoulders and felt her melt.

"I'm still not clear about your motives," she said. "And I'm not sure I support them, either."

"I'm certain you don't," Jerry stared idly at the bishop's flesh as little ripples ran from the back of his pink neck, over his grey bottom and down his legs. "You've tired him out."

She kissed his shoulder and wriggled against his coat. "It wasn't hard."

"I could see that." Still, thought Jerry, it was a shame to see the great predator brought low.

"What's it got to do with the Committee?" she asked.

"Well, I can't beat it. Not at present. And I don't want to join it. I've seen enough of it. It gets so boring. Besides it won't last that long. But while it does it will re-introduce so much in the way of guilt that the next era's bound to get off to a slower start than I'd have liked. I still indulge these visions of Utopia, you see." He waved a hand at the bishop. "A lesson in tolerance."

"I didn't know you were interested in politics."

"I'm not. This is an artistic impulse. Like Bukaninism." He sniffed. "I've a horror of the Law of Precedent. It's bad logic. Could you put the new Hawkwind album on?"

While she went into the next room he swallowed a couple of tabs of speed.

The music began to fill the room. She came back and she was looking lovely. He smiled at her.

"We've got to struggle on somehow," he said. "Everything

fades. Only love can conquer disintegration. Only love denies the Second Law of Thermodynamics. Love love, it's the best thing we have." Jerry groaned as she fell upon him, biting and caressing. "Oh, my love! Oh, my love!"

It took her five long minutes to unbuckle his belt. While she did it he reflected that if he'd achieved nothing else he had almost certainly re-programmed Beesley. It was bound to make a difference. A small victory was all he had a right to expect at this stage.

8

Jerry's mum was furious. "Wot they wanna call it a bloody 'Forbidden Sector' for, then?" She put down her bag on a pile of newspapers. "I was aht shoppin' when I saw 'em putting up the fuckin' barbed wire. I asked the bloke. – 'It's 'cause of all them prossies,' 'e says. 'Fuck that!' I says – 'Wot abaht the decent people?' – 'Yer can always move aht,' 'e says. Well, fuck that! Anyway, Jer' – they're lookin' for *you*. Wotcher bin up to? Don' tell me." She lowered herself into her armchair and kicked her shoes off. Jerry poured her a cup of tea.

"I just made it," he said.

She became nervous. "Thinkin' of stayin' 'ere?"

He shook his head. "Just want to change my appearance a bit, then I'll be off."

"Be as well," she said. "Yore not lookin' too chipper."

"I've had a busy time."

"Boys!" she said. "Give me girls any day of the week. They're a lot less trouble."

"Well, I suppose it's all a question of circumstances."

"Too right!" She offered him a look that was a mixture of affection and introspection. "It's a man's world, innit?"

Jerry had discarded his gear and was now dressed in the dark blue suit he usually wore to his mum's.

"You got a good place to go to?" she asked.

"It'll do."

"Not to worry. Everythin' blows over."

"Let's hope so."

"Your trouble is, Jerry, yore too fuckin' confident and then you get too fuckin' low. Yore dad was the same. I've 'ardly known a man that wasn't. All puff and strut one minute and like a little kid the next. Men. Want yore own way all the time. Then when you don't get it . . ."

"I know, Mum."

"It's women that suffers, Jerry." She gave a satisfied sniff.

Jerry sighed and reached down to pick up his suitcase. "I know. Well, I'll just go and change. Then I'll be off."

When he reappeared in the kitchen he was wearing his midi-skirt, his Jaeger sweater, his court shoes, his auburn wig, his pearls. Mrs Cornelius screeched. Her body shook and tears of laughter filled her eyes. Sweat brightened her forehead. "Cor!" She gasped and paused. "Yore full o' surprises, Jerry. You shoulda bin in showbiz. That's a disguise and an 'alf all right!"

"It always was," said Jerry. He blew her a kiss and left.

Outside, Mo was waiting in the Mercedes. The armour plates were in position at most of the windows. Mo had a Banning Mark Four on the floor beside the passenger seat. He patted the big gun as he got the car moving. Jerry settled himself in the back. It was dusk and the first searchlight beams of the evening were already swinging over the grey streets.

"Time for some business, Mr C?"

"Get you," said Jerry. He noticed that his left stocking had started to run. He wetted his finger and dabbed at the ladder. "You can't win them all."

The Mercedes jumped forward. Jerry cradled his own Banning, stroking its cool metal barrel, working its action back and forth. There was an explosion to the west, near Ladbroke Grove, a short burst of machine-gun fire. Jerry saw a tank cross the street at the intersection just ahead of them.

"At least it's simpler than sex." He began to load the Banning.

"And a bloody sight more fun!" Mo grinned wound down the window and lobbed a grenade at a sub-post office. There was a flash, a bang and a lot of glass flew about.

"Here we go again, Mr C."

The Entropy Circuit

1

Cosmology

"It is impossible to guess what the human race will do in the next ten years . . ."

Everything was getting sluggish.

Jerry Cornelius: stumbling upon the boards of his bare bed-sitter; trying to find water for his consumptive girl-wife who coughed, heated and naked, under the thin grey sheet; who trembled. He would have been glad of a drink, something to smoke, a tab of limbitrol, perhaps.

The water in the jug was low and warm. He found a cup.

unable to see in the gloom if it was clean, and poured. He stopped, jug in hand, staring through the cracks and the grime of the window at the unlit, deserted street, reviewing suddenly the future, contemplating the past, unwilling to consider a present which at that moment appeared to have betrayed him. A wind moved the palms flanking the avenue; the sea, unseen, the Mediterranean, gasped against the shingle below the promenade on to which the pension fronted. It was winter and Jerry had been waiting in Menton since the previous summer.

Jerry returned to the bed, offering the cup, but she was asleep again; her light snores were uneven, sickly. He drank and turned to the table; it was covered in papers, abandoned forms. Nearly a year ago he had set off for the Vatican with a plan owing more to drug euphoria than to logic, knowing nothing of the new regulations limiting border traffic into Italy from France. Here, in Menton, he had planned to stay a couple of nights at most, but first he had had to wait for a new benzine permit (it had not been granted and his postal request to London had been unacknowledged). Later, trying to cross into San Remo on foot he had been informed that passage was granted on certain days only, each case being considered individually, and he would need a visa. It had taken a month for the visa to arrive and during that time there had come further restrictions; the border had been opened with only a day's warning in advance, five times in the past six months, and the rule was simply first come, first served. If you stood in line, there was a chance that you would be allowed to cross (barring official disapproval) before the barrier came down again. Twice Jerry had got as close as ten or fifteen people before the line had been turned away; three times he had failed to hear the news that the border was to be opened. In attempting to conserve his various resources, he had not followed the example of other travellers and tried, fruitlessly, to find a less heavily trafficked crossing point, but now he was running out of cash, and he had little left to sell.

He touched the stud of his Pulsar watch; the numerals seemed to glow more faintly and soon the power cell would give out altogether, for all that he had made every effort to preserve it as long as possible. The red numerals said 5.46; he released the stud before the seconds had time to register. He wondered if Mo Collier would be able to get here in time. Mo had promised to smuggle some money through to him, if he could. He knew that he was luckier than many; he had seen the pathetic tents and shanties in the hills above the town; he had seen the corpses on the coast road near the entrance to the tunnel; he had seen the children who had been left behind.

He shuffled the papers and found Mo's postcard again. It had taken over three weeks to arrive and read: "Wish you were here, Mr C. Should be taking a holiday myself in a month or so." Checking the London postmark, Jerry had worked out that this could put the time of Mo's arrival within the fortnight since he had received it. Turning over one of several spoiled forms, he came across some lines written either by himself or the girl he had married in Menton on Christmas Day (there had been a rumour, then, since discounted, that married couples received preferential treatment at the border):

"The power of love is harder to sustain
By far than that easy instrument
The brutal power of pain."

His lips moved as he stared at the sheet; he frowned, plucking at the frayed cuff of his black car coat. Were the words a quotation; had he or the girl been inspired to write them down? He was unable to interpret them. He screwed the paper up and let it fall amongst its fellows.

He folded his arms against an unanticipated chill.

2

Cosmogonies

"The first principle of the universe to take form was Cronos, or Time, which came out of Chaos, symbolising the infinite, and Ether, symbolising the finite."

"It's all falling apart, Jerry," said Shaky Mo Collier as he handed over the last of the cash (each £1 overstamped to the value of £100). "Sorry it had to be sterling. How much longer can it go on for? A few million years and nobody will have heard of the

South of France, or Brighton, for that matter. I know I'm in a gloomy mood – but who *has* got the energy these days? That's what I'd like to know."

Jerry held up his heater. The ray of watery sunlight from the window fell on it. "Here's some, for a start."

"And what did it cost you?"

"Oh, well . . ." Jerry looked in the mirror at the bags under his eyes, the lines on his face. "That's entropy for you."

"I brought you some petrol, too," said Mo.

"How did you get it through?"

Mo was pleased with himself. "It's in spare tanks, in the tanks themselves. It's worth twice the value of the car, for all it looks very flash on the outside. I'm going to get a boat from Marseilles, first chance."

"Going straight back?"

"Straight? That's a laugh, these days."

The girl was better today. Coughing only a little, she moved slowly from the lavatory and back to the bed. She tried to smile at Mo, who winked at Jerry. "Doing all right, still, I see."

"We pooled our resources." Jerry felt he should explain.

"I know what you mean." Another wink.

With a sigh the girl got into the bed and pulled the sheet around her thin body. She pushed back dirty fair hair from her oval face while, with her other hand, she fumbled for cigarettes and matches on the bamboo table beside her. She struck a match. It failed to light. She struck another and the same thing happened. After several tries, she abandoned the box. Mo stepped forward, snapping a gold Dunhill lighter. Nothing happened.

"That's funny," he said. "It was working okay this morning." He peered at it, flicking the wheel. "Not a spark. But the flint's new."

Aggrieved, but at the same time reconciled, Mo replaced the lighter in his pocket. He glanced at his watch. "Oh, shit," he said, "that's fucking stopped as well."

Jerry murmured an apology.

Mo said: "It's not your fucking fault, Jerry. Not really. Or is it?"

There was a knock on the thin wood of the door. Quickly,

Jerry opened the drawer in the table and slipped the tight wad of notes into it. "Come in."

It was Miss Brunner. She was precisely clothed, in a dark blue tweed costume. She looked disdainfully at Mo's long, greasy hair, his untidy moustache, his dirty denims, but when she saw Jerry and the condition of his room, she smiled with genuine relish. "My, you have come down in the world."

"I think that's true of most of us. What brings you to Menton out of season?"

"You can't afford to be sulky, I'd have thought." She cast a cool eye at the girl. "Or choosy, it seems. I heard you were hard up, stuck, in trouble. I came to help."

Mo moved uneasily, making for the door. "Well, I'll be seeing you, Jerry. You don't want me . . . ?"

"Take it easy, Mo."

Mo allowed himself a quick, almost cheerful grin. "What there is left to take, Mr C. I hope things work out. Keep in touch."

As the door closed, Miss Brunner stopped her speculative eyeing of the girl and turned to Jerry. "I've a job," she said, "which could solve all your problems. Would you like the details? What about your friend?"

"Don't worry about her," said Jerry. He stood beside the girl, stroking her soft cheek. "She's dying."

"You were on your way to the Vatican, I heard."

"A year ago. I was getting used to it here, though."

"This would take you to the Vatican. You know it's been closed off for months – hardly anyone allowed in or out. Why were you going? Somebody offer you work?"

"It sounded tasty."

"I got an offer, too – on the computer. But I wanted complete autonomy. Anyway, I heard what they're up to and it would, I think, be mutually convenient if you were to throw a spanner or two in the works."

"Mutually convenient? Who else is involved?"

"I'm representing a consortium."

"Beesley?"

"He has special reasons for being interested in the project," she admitted.

"Maxwell."

"Oh, you don't have to name them all, Mr Cornelius."

"The usual gang, in fact. I'm not sure. Every time I've thrown in my lot with you I've come out of it – "

"Wiser," she said. "And that's the main thing. Besides, we haven't always won."

"It's spending the time that I mind. And the energy."

"In this case, if you're successful, you get all you need of both."

She explained what she thought was happening at the Vatican.

3

Fundamentals

"Probably the most extraordinary coincidence discovered by science is the fact that the basic formulae for three separate, and apparently unrelated, energy systems are almost identical."

It was good to be on the road again, though the forty-five-kilometre speed limit didn't exactly make for a zippy trip. Sitting beside him as they negotiated the winding coast road beyond Genoa, the girl looked almost healthy. She had the window of the Ambassador station wagon all the way down and a light rain fell on her bare arm.

"We can only be kind to one another," she said, "there is scarcely any alternative if we are to resist chaos."

Jerry was saved from replying by the stereo's groan, indicating that the tape was running too slow. It had been getting worse and worse. He tugged the cartridge from the player and turned the radio on long enough to hear a few bars of some song for Europe. He despaired. He switched it off. Behind them, in the drizzle, the grey, square towers of Genoa were overshadowed by huge neon signs showing stylised pictures of rats and warning them to be vigilant for new plagues.

"Love among the predators," said Jerry reminiscently. "Is this your first trip to Rome?"

"Oh, no," she said. "My last."

Their surroundings widened out. On their right they could see the remains of a small hillside town which had been burned in an effort to contain a plague.

"The world's filling up with fucking metaphors." Jerry kept his eyes on the road. "Too fucking many metaphors."

4

Universe

"To the old ones, the sun was energy or god or both, but the stars were different."

The car padded through the wet streets of the Roman night as Jerry sought the address Miss Brunner had given him; without any kind of street lighting, it was almost impossible to read the signs, for the moon appeared only intermittently through the heavy cloud. Police cars, impressed by the size of the station wagon, were curious, but left him alone. There were even more police in Rome now. During Jerry's last trip the various kinds of policemen had at last begun to outnumber the male civilians in the city.

Someone had been standing in a doorway and began to approach when they saw the car, flagging it down. Jerry pulled in to the side, touching the control panel on his door to lower the left front window (the girl had fallen asleep).

"Still managing to keep up appearances, then," said the man in the trenchcoat. It was his brother Frank, seedy as ever. He leered in. "Going to give me a lift, Jerry? I've been waiting for you."

Jerry leaned across and opened the rear door. Frank climbed in with a sigh and began to unbutton his coat. The faint smell of mould filled the car.

Frank rubbed comfortably at his stubble. "It's like old times, again."

"You said it," said Jerry despondently.

"Make a right," said Frank. "Then a left. How long is it since you were welcome at the Vatican?"

"Quite a while." Jerry followed the instructions. They went over the river.

"Head for St Peter's."

The girl woke up, sniffing. "Dope?" she murmured.

"Frank," said Jerry.

"This'll do," Frank told him. They stopped by a toy-shop; they were about a hundred yards from the Vatican City.

Frank left the car and let himself into the toy-shop. Jerry and the girl followed. At last, as they reached the back of the shop, Jerry recognised where he was.

Frank grinned. "That's right. One of your old hot-spots. And the tunnel's been re-activated. We were lucky. Most of the catacombs are filled up with stolen cars, these days. It's conservation, of sorts, I suppose." He pulled aside a gigantic, soft bear to reveal a hole in the wall. Taking a flashlight from his pocket, he led the way.

Within a few moments they had descended into ancient darkness. Frank's thin beam touched the carved face of Mithras. Jerry glared back at it. He considered it a poor likeness.

5

God

"There is no figure in modern developed societies to compare
  with that of the shaman."

Jerry's boots crushed the gross, leprous toadstools which grew between the cracks in the flagstones; their smell reminding him of Frank, their flesh of Bishop Beesley, their toxicity of Miss Brunner, all of whom now stood in the chamber at the end of the tunnel, together with Captain Maxwell, the Protestant engineer, his huge backside turned towards Jerry as he fiddled with a piece of equipment.

"It's got a lot warmer, at any rate." Jerry noticed that his watch burned brighter; the girl's face had lost its pallor.

"That's because we're under the bloody Vatican," said Frank. "Well, is it a complete set, Miss Brunner?"

"It would have been nice to have had Doktor von Krupp, but

she's faded away altogether, I'm afraid. A termination, we can safely say."

Most of the equipment in the chamber was familiar to Jerry.

Captain Maxwell straightened up, wiping sticky sweat from his choleric features. He pursed his lips when he saw Jerry, but made no comment. "She's still acting up a bit," he told Miss Brunner. "Perhaps we could try a modified programme?"

"That would take us back to square one," she said.

Jerry said: "It looks like we're there already."

"It's our last chance." Unexpectedly, her tone was defensive.

"I'd say His Holiness has already beaten you." Jerry wondered at his own glow of satisfaction; previously, he had always been inclined to associate their consortium with that of the Papal Palace. "He's got the brains, the equipment, the power."

"Not all of it, Mr Cornelius." Bishop Beesley unwrapped an Italian chocolate bar. "I think I speak for everyone here when I say we've no time for your brand of cynicism, and I might remind you that *we* have the experience. Besides," he added with a smirk, indicating a tangle of thick cables disappearing into a hole in the ceiling, "we're tapping a lot of his resources."

"Undetected?"

"The energy situation throughout the world is so unstable," Miss Brunner told him, "that they're putting the fluctuation down to the increased entropy rate."

"You know how mystical people can get about energy," said Frank. "That's where we have the edge on them. Half their problems are semantic – there's a lot of confusion just because most of their people can't distinguish between the specific meanings of, well, 'energy'."

"They're still thrashing about in a lot of metaphors," said Miss Brunner.

"I know how they feel," said Jerry.

6

Body

"While questions of origin tickle the imagination, they are, on the whole, insoluble."

Jerry glanced idly at the dials, but he was impressed. "He's certainly accumulating energy at a pretty fast lick. You know what he's using it for, do you? Specifically?"

"He's just trying to consolidate. It's a human enough ambition in times like these." Miss Brunner ran a pale hand over a console. "After all, it's only what we're aiming for."

"I think it's greedy," said the girl.

Miss Brunner sighed and turned away.

Frank wasn't upset by the remark. "It's the logical extension of capitalist philosophy," he said. He moistened his lips with his tongue. His eyes were already wet, and hot. Jerry could tell he was trying to be agreeable.

"God knows what would happen if this lot blew." Captain Maxwell could not disguise the note of glee in his voice. "Boom!"

Jerry was beginning to regret his weakness in throwing in with them.

"It's the Pope's last bid for divinity, I suppose," said Bishop Beesley enviously. "That's why we've got to stop him. And that's why we need you, Mr Cornelius, as a – um – ?"

"Hit man," supplied Frank. "With the Pope knocked over, they'll never get round to sussing us. We know you've got a lot of other talents, Jerry, but, well, we've got Miss Brunner's computer doing your old job, and this was the only other opening."

Captain Maxwell put an affectionate hand on the machine. "Standard Hexamerous and Multiple Axis Noumena," he said.

Jerry stared at him in astonishment. "What a load of rubbish."

"You work it out," said Miss Brunner. "Anyway, I think we're all too grown up for silly jealousies, don't you? The fact is, you agreed to do a job."

"I thought you wanted . . . ?"

"Your noumena? You must realise, Mr Cornelius, that you're getting a bit stale." She became sentimental. "You've done a lot of interesting work in your time, but you're past thirty now. Face up to it. You ought to be glad of any work." She reached out a hand, but he avoided it. "How much longer could you have lasted in Menton? You were fading yourself."

"I think I'll go back to Menton, just the same."

"You won't find much of it left," she said with a self-satisfied smirk. "I had to pull all sorts of strings to get you out, not to mention the deals I made with the French governments."

"You'll have everything we can give you, to help," said Bishop Beesley encouragingly. "We're diverting a whole section of the grid for your use alone."

Jerry shrugged. He had avoided the knowledge for too long. Now he didn't care. He was a has-been. "I'll need some music," he murmured pathetically.

"Oh, we've got all your old favourites." Frank presented him with a case of tapes.

7

World

"Until Elizabethan days there had been a comparatively low level of national energy consumption."

Jerry and the girl climbed the cracked steps, side by side. She was dressed as a nun, a Poor Clare; he was in his old Jesuit kit. The steps ended suddenly and Jerry pushed at the panel which blocked their way. They saw that the corridor beyond the panel was deserted and they climbed out, dusting down their habits. Jerry pushed the Rubens back into place. They found themselves surrounded by the tatty opulence, the vulgarity, of the Papal Palace itself. Commenting on it in a murmur, Jerry added: "It was the main reason I finally copped out. Of course I was much younger then. And idealistic, I suppose."

"Still," she said consolingly, "they offered you the research facilities you needed."

"Oh, yes," he agreed, "I'm not knocking it." He was pleased by the irony, that his last caper should take place where his first had begun. There would be no chance of resurrection, if his plans worked out.

Two cardinals went by, carrying small pieces of electronic gear. They whispered as they walked. As he and the girl approached a small side door, Jerry took some keys from his pocket. He stopped by the door, selected a key and slid it into the lock.

It turned. They went into a cramped, circular room with a high ceiling.

The room was furnished with three chairs in gilt and purple plush, a brass table. On the table was a telephone. Jerry picked up the receiver, pausing until a voice answered in good, but affected, Italian.

"Could you tell him Cornelius is here?" asked Jerry politely, in English. He replaced the receiver and turned to the girl. "We might as well sit down."

They waited in silence for nearly half-an-hour before the Pope arrived through the other door. His thin lips were curved in a smile, his thin hands embraced one of Jerry's. "So you made it, after all. You're not feeling good, Jerry?" He laughed. "You look almost as old as me. And that's pretty old, eh? Is this your assistant?"

"Yes," said Jerry.

"My child." He acknowledged the girl who was staring at him in some astonishment; he spoke again to Jerry: "There isn't much time." He sighed, sitting down in the vacant chair. "Ah, Jerry, I had such hopes for you, such faith. For a while I thought you were really Him . . ." He chuckled, dismissing his regrets. "But you passed your chance, eh?"

"Maybe the next time round."

"This is the last ride on the circuit for all of us, I fear."

"That's my guess, too," Jerry agreed. "Still, we've had a good run."

"Better than most."

Jerry told him what was happening in the catacombs.

8

Earth

"The solar wind also distorts the magnetic field."

Miss Brunner snarled. "Judas!" she said. She had a Swiss Guard holding a naked arm each. "Oh, you revert to type, you Corneliuses."

"Common as muck," agreed Captain Maxwell, his accent thickening.

"Do you mind?" asked Frank. He had been allowed to keep his raincoat on after it had been revealed what lay beneath it.

"Is there any chance of getting our clothes back, Your Holiness?" The bishop's tones were plummy and placatory.

"In your case," said the Pope with a wave of his hand which made his rings sparkle, "I'm not sure."

"I hope," said Captain Maxwell, "that you don't think we were deliberately . . ."

"Stealing my power?" The Pope shrugged. "It's an instinct with you, Captain – like a rat stealing grain. I don't blame you, but I might have to pray for you."

Maxwell shuddered.

"You are altruistic, Your Holiness," began Bishop Beesley conversationally, "and I am sure you recognise altruism in others. We are interested in the pursuit of knowledge for its own sake. It never occurred to us that we were so close to the Vatican City. If we had known . . ."

Only Miss Brunner preserved silence, listening with some amusement to her colleagues' patently unconvincing lies; she contented herself with the odd glare in Jerry's direction.

The Pope settled himself comfortably in his throne. "In a case of this kind, I'm afraid that the old-fashioned methods seem to be the best."

"You'll make a lovely Joan of Arc," said Jerry, but he was not really happy with the course that events had taken. He was feeling very lively, thanks to the transference jolts they had given him before they sent him on his mission.

"There's nothing in this for you, Mr Cornelius," said Miss Brunner. "I hope that's clear. You're all used up."

"Recriminations aside," murmured the Pope, rising again, "I think I've worked out a practical scheme which should secure your repentance and further our own work here. Forgive me if I admit to having a concern for expediencies; my office demands it from me. Few of us can survive the present crisis, and it's my job to ensure the continuance of the Faith, by whatever means are available to me."

"You people would pervert technology to the most superstitious, the most primitive ends imaginable." Miss Brunner turned her rage upon the old man. "At least I had the cause of Science at heart. And that," directing her attention to Jerry once more, "is what you've betrayed, Mr Cornelius."

"Ah," said the Pope, "come in, my son."

A fat Indian teenager waddled in. He had the dazed, self-important air of the partially lobotomised. "The fog is getting thicker," he explained. "My plane was delayed. Hello, Mr Cornelius."

"Guru." Jerry took a packet of cigarettes from his cassock. "Got a light?"

The Indian boy sighed and ignored the request. "How does our work progress, Your Holiness?"

"I think we can expect it to go much faster now. For that we must thank Mr Cornelius." The Pope beamed at Jerry. "You will not be forgotten. This could mean a canonisation for you. Better than nothing, eh?" He signed to the guards. "Please take the prisoners down to the input room."

9

Mind

"But when it comes to psychological activity which *apparently* involves no physical movement whatsoever, we are hard pressed to state a satisfactory cause or energy source."

An hour later, when he accompanied his new friends to the input room, Jerry found it hard to recognise his own brother, let alone the others. They all had the anonymity of the very old, the very senile. They quivered a little and made the electrode leads shimmy on their way to the central accumulator, but otherwise they were incapable of movement. Bishop Beesley's loose skin hung on his body like an old overcoat. Somewhere in the background came the sounds of The Deep Fix playing *Funeral March*, a big hit in the mid-seventies. This was by no means the first time Jerry had seen them die, but this was certainly the most convincing death he had witnessed.

Miss Brunner's washed-out eyes located him, but it was not

certain that she had recognised him. Her shrunken lips moved, her grey skin twitched.

Jerry began to walk towards her, but the Pope held him back and went forward himself, cupping his hand around his ear as he bent to listen to her. He straightened up, an expression of gentle satisfaction upon his carefully cosmeticised features. "She repents," he said. The machines clicked and muttered, as if in approval.

Jerry took out his heater and gunned the guards down before they could lift their old-fashioned M-16s into position.

"So you don't stand for Religion, either," said the Pope. He fingered the complicated crucifix at his throat. "And you don't stand for Science. You stand for nothing, Jerry. You are alone. Are you sure you have the courage for that?" He took a step, reaching a hand towards the gun. "Consider . . ."

Jerry shot him through the crucifix. He sat down on the clean floor.

The Indian teenager's face bore the calm of absolute fear, a familiar expression which many, in the past, had mistaken for tranquillity of mind. He spoke mechanically. "You must love something."

"I love her," said Jerry, with a movement of his head in the direction of the girl who stood uncertainly by the door. "And Art," he added with some embarrassment, "the foundation for both your houses." He grinned. "This is for Art's sake."

He shot the boy in his fat little heart. He put his gun away and drew the bomb from his cassock, activating it as he slapped it against the metal of the nearest machine. "It's beautiful equipment," he said regretfully, "but it's useless now."

He took the girl's hand in his and led her from the room. They did not hurry as they made their way back to the passage behind the Rubens, through the tunnel, through the toy-shop and out into the dawn street.

He helped her into the car. "How are you feeling?"

She dismissed his concern. "Can you justify so much violence?"

He got into the driving seat and started the car. "No," he said, "but it's become a question of degrees, these days, hasn't it? Besides, I'm an egalitarian at heart."

"Won't this mean chaos?"

"It depends what you mean by chaos." He drove steadily, at forty-five kph, towards the outskirts of the city. The rain had stopped and a pale, gold sun was rising in a cloudless sky. "To the fearful all things are chaotic. That's how you get religion (and its bastard child, politics)."

"And science, too?"

"Their kind."

She shook her head. "I'm not convinced."

He laughed, speeding up as they took the road to Tivoli, passing the ruined façades of a dozen defunct film studios. "Neither am I."

Behind them, Rome was burning. Jerry checked the position of the sun, he opened his window and threw the gun into the road. He kissed her. Then he began to head East. With a sigh, she closed her eyes and sank back into sleep.

(All quotes from *An Index of Possibilities*)

The End